"You can have two months, but not a day more," she said.

Staring at the oh-so-hot naked man in her bed, McKenzie clutched the sheet to her. *Please agree with me*, she pleaded silently. She couldn't fathom not repeating the magic she'd just experienced, but she would do just that if he didn't agree.

Already she was risking too much. She didn't want a future that might lead her down the path her parents had taken. Bachelorettehood was the life for her, all the way. Hearing Lance agree that they'd end things in two months was necessary for them to carry on. She wouldn't—couldn't—risk anything longer.

"Promise me," she urged.

"Two months sounds absolutely perfect," he said.

Dear Reader,

Christmas time is here! I'm so blessed to be able to write another Christmas story. I love the holidays *and* romance, so what could be better than combining the two?

Dr Lance Spencer is a hero I immediately fell for. Kind, generous, fun, witty and a bit tortured, he stole my heart. Unfortunately it takes him a while to win over my heroine. Then again, McKenzie's an independent woman who knows what she wants in life—and it *isn't* to be tied down to a man. But the holidays sure are a lot more fun with Lance at her side, so McKenzie agrees to a two-month relationship that leads them down a path that ultimately makes *every* day feel like Christmas.

I hope you enjoy their story as much as I enjoyed writing it. As always, I enjoy hearing from my readers at Janice@janicelynn.net. Happy Holidays—and I hope Santa is good to you!

Love,

Janice

IT STARTED
AT CHRISTMAS...

BY
JANICE LYNN

Published in Great Britain 2016
By Mills & Boon, an imprint of HarperCollins*Publishers*
1 London Bridge Street, London, SE1 9GF

Our policy is to use papers that are natural, renewable and recyclable

Janice Lynn has a Master's in Nursing from Vanderbilt University, and works as a nurse practitioner in a family practice. She lives in the southern United States with her husband, their four children, their Jack Russell—appropriately named Trouble—and a lot of unnamed dust bunnies that have moved in since she started her writing career. To find out more about Janice and her writing visit janicelynn.com.

Books by Janice Lynn

Mills & Boon Medical Romance

The Doctor's Damsel in Distress
Flirting with the Society Doctor
Challenging the Nurse's Rules
NYC Angels: Heiress's Baby Scandal
The ER's Newest Dad
After the Christmas Party...
Flirting with the Doc of Her Dreams
New York Doc to Blushing Bride
Winter Wedding in Vegas
Sizzling Nights with Dr Off-Limits

Visit the Author Profile page at millsandboon.co.uk for more titles.

Janice won The National Readers' Choice Award for her first book
The Doctor's Pregnancy Bombshell

To Blake Shelton for Retweeting me
following his Nashville concert and giving me
a total fangirl rush moment. Life is good.

CHAPTER ONE

"OKAY, WHO'S THE HUNK that just winked at you?"

At her best friend's question Dr. McKenzie Sanders rolled her eyes at the emcee stepping out onto the Coopersville Community Theater stage. "That's him."

"That's the infamous Dr. Lance Spencer?" Cecilia sounded incredulous from the chair next to McKenzie's.

No wonder. Her best friend had heard quite a bit about the doctor slash local charity advocate. Was there any local charity he wasn't involved with in some shape, form or fashion? McKenzie doubted it.

Still, when he'd invited her to come and watch the Christmas program, she'd not been expecting the well-choreographed show currently playing out before her eyes. Lance and his crew were good. Then again, knowing Lance, she should have expected greatness. He'd put the event together and everything the man touched was pure perfection.

And these days he wanted to touch her.

Sometimes McKenzie wondered if it was a case of women-chasing-him-toward-the-holy-matrimony-altar burnout that had him focusing on commitment-phobic her. She never planned to marry and Lance knew it. She made no secret of the fact she was a good-time girl and was never going to be tied down by the golden band of death to all future happiness. After his last girlfriend had gone a little psycho when he'd told her flat out he had no intention of ever proposing, Lance apparently wanted a break from tall lanky blonde numbers trying to drag him into wedded "bliss." He'd taken to chasing petite brunettes who got hives at the mere mention of marriage thanks to unhappily divorced parents.

Her.

Despite accepting his invitation and hauling Cecilia with her to watch his show, McKenzie was running as fast as she could and had no intention of letting Lance "catch" her. She didn't want a relationship with him, other than their professional one and the light, fun friendship they already shared. Something else she'd learned from her parents thanks to her dad, who'd chased every female coworker he'd ever had. McKenzie was nothing like either of her parents. Still, she could appreciate fineness when she saw it.

Lance was fine with a capital F.

Especially in his suit that appeared tailor-made.

Lance was no doubt one of those men who crawled out of bed covered in nonstop sexy. He was that kind of guy. The kind who made you want to skip that heavily iced cupcake and do some sit-ups instead just in case he ever saw you naked. The kind McKenzie avoided because she was a free spirit who wasn't going to change herself for any man. Not ever. She'd eat her cupcake and have another if she wanted, with extra icing, thank you very much.

She'd watched women change for a man, seen her own mother do that, time and again. Ultimately, the changes didn't last, the men lost interest, and the women involved ended up with broken hearts and a lot of confusion about who they were. McKenzie never gave any man a chance to get close enough to change her. She dated, had a good time and a good life. When things started getting sticky, she moved on. Next, please.

Really, she and Lance had a lot in common in that regard. Except he usually dated the same woman for several months and McKenzie's relationships never lasted more than a few weeks at best. Anything longer than that just gave guys the wrong idea.

Like that she might be interested in white picket fences, a soccer-mom minivan, two point five kids, and a husband who would quickly get bored with her and have flirtations with his secretary…his therapist…his accountant…his law firm partner's wife…his children's schoolteacher…and who knew who else her father had cheated on her mother with?

Men cheated. It was a fact of life.

Sure, there were probably a few good ones out there still if she wanted to search for that needle in a haystack. McKenzie didn't.

She wouldn't change for a man or allow him to run around on her while she stayed home and scrubbed his bathroom floor and wiped his kids' snotty noses. No way. She'd enjoy life, enjoy the opposite sex, and never make the mistake of being like her mother…or her father, who obviously couldn't be faithful yet seemed to think he needed a wife on hand at all times since he'd just walked down the aisle for the fourth time since his divorce from McKenzie's mother.

Which made her question why she'd said no to Lance when he'd asked her out.

Sure, there was the whole working-together thing that she clung to faithfully due to being scarred for life by her dad's office romantic endeavors. Still, it wasn't as if either she or Lance would be in it for anything more than to have some fun together. She was a fun-loving woman. He was a fun-loving man. They'd have fun together. Of that, she had no doubt. They were friends and occasionally hung out in groups of friends or shared a quick meal at the hospital. He managed to make her smile even on her toughest days. But when it had come to actually dating him she'd scurried away faster than a mouse in the midst of a spinster lady's feline-filled house.

"Emcee got your tongue?" Cecilia asked, making McKenzie realize she hadn't answered her friend, neither had she caught most of what Lance had said as she'd gotten lost in a whirlwind of the past and present.

"Sorry, I'm feeling a little distracted," she shot back under her breath, her eyes on Lance and not the woman watching her intently.

"I just bet you are." Cecilia laughed softly and, although McKenzie still didn't turn to look at her friend, she could imagine the merriment that was no doubt sparkling in her friend's warm brown eyes. "That man is so hot I think I feel a fever coming on. I might need some medical care very soon. What's his specialty?"

"Internal medicine, not that you don't already know that seeing as he works with me," McKenzie pointed out, her gaze eating up Lance as he announced the first act, taking in the fluid movements of his body, the smile on his face, the dimples in his cheeks, the twinkle in his blue eyes. He looked like a movie star. He was a great doctor. What else could he do?

McKenzie gulped back the knot forming in her throat as her imagination took flight on the possibilities.

"Yeah, well, Christmas is all about getting a fabulous package, right? That man, right there, is a fabulous package," Cecilia teased, nudging McKenzie's arm.

Snorting, she rolled her eyes and hoped her friend couldn't see the heat flooding her cheeks. "You have a one-track mind."

"So do you and it's not usually on men. You still competing in that marathon in the morning?"

Running. It's what McKenzie did. She ran. Every morning. It's how she cleared her head. How she brought in each new day. How she stayed one step ahead of any guy who tried to wiggle his way into her heart or bedroom. She ran.

Literally and figuratively.

Not that she was a virgin. She wasn't. Her innocence had run away a long time ago, too. It was just that she was choosy about who she let touch her body.

Which brought her right back to the man onstage wooing the audience with his smile and charm.

He wanted to touch her body. Not that he'd said those exact words out loud. It was in how he looked at her.

He looked at her as if he couldn't bear not to look at her.

As if he'd like to tear her clothes off and show her why she should hang up her running shoes for however long the chemistry held out.

She gulped again and forced more of those possibilities out of her mind.

Loud applause sounded around the dinner theater as the show moved from one song to the next. Before long, Lance introduced a trio of females who sang a song about getting nothing for Christmas. At the end of the trio's set, groups of carolers made their way around the room, singing near the tables rather than on the stage. Lance remained just off to the side of the stage and was directly in her line of vision. His gaze met hers and he grinned. Great, he'd caught her staring at him. Then again, wasn't that why he'd invited her to attend?

Because he wanted her to watch him.

She winced. Doggone her because seeing him outside the clinic made her watch. She didn't want to watch him... only she did want to watch. And to feel. And to...

Cecilia elbowed her, and not with the gentle nudge as before.

"Ouch." She rubbed her arm and frowned. No way could her friend have read her mind and even if she had, she was pretty sure Cecilia would be high-fiving her and not dishing out reprimands.

"Just wanted to make sure you were seeing what I'm seeing, because he can't seem to keep his gaze off you."

"I'm not blind," she countered, still massaging the sore spot on her arm.

"After seeing the infamous Dr. Spencer I've heard you talk about so much and that I know you've said no to, I'm beginning to think perhaps you are. How long has it been since you last saw an optometrist?"

"Ha-ha, you're so funny. There's more to life than good looks." Okay, so Lance was hot and she'd admit her body responded to that hotness. Always had. But even if there wasn't her whole-won't-date-a-coworker rule, she enjoyed her working relationship with Lance. If they dated, she didn't fool herself for one second that they wouldn't end up in bed. Then what? They weren't going to be having a happily ever after. Work would become awkward. Did she really want to deal with all that just for a few weeks of sexy Lance this Christmas season?

Raking her gaze over him, she could almost convince herself it would be worth it…almost.

"Yeah," Cecilia agreed. "There's that voice that I could listen to all night long. Sign me up for a hefty dose of some of that."

"Just because he has this crowd, and you, eating out of the palm of his hand, it doesn't mean I should go out with him."

Cecilia's face lit with amusement. "What about you? Are you included in those he has eating out of the palm of his hand? Because I'm thinking you should. Literally."

She didn't. She wouldn't. She couldn't.

"I was just being a smart aleck," McKenzie countered.

"Yeah, I know." Cecilia ran her gaze over where Lance

caroled, dressed up in old-fashioned garb and top hat. "But I'm serious. He could be the one."

Letting out a long breath, McKenzie shook her head. "You know better than that."

Cecilia had been her best friend since kindergarten. She'd been with McKenzie through all life's ups and downs. Now McKenzie was a family doctor in a small group of physicians and Cecilia was a hairdresser at Bev's Beauty Boutique. They'd both grown up to be what they'd always wanted to be. Except Cecilia was still waiting for her Prince Charming to come along and sweep her off her feet and across the threshold. Silly girl.

McKenzie was a big girl and could walk across that threshold all by herself. No Prince Charming needed or wanted.

Her gaze shifted from her friend and back to Lance. He was watching her. She'd swear he'd smiled at her. Maybe it was just the sparkle in his eyes that made her think that. Maybe.

Or maybe it went back to what she'd been thinking moments before about how the man looked at her. He made her want to let him look. It made her feel uncomfortable. Very uncomfortable.

Which was probably part of why she kept telling him no.

Only she was here tonight.

Why?

"I think you should go for it."

She blinked at Cecilia. "It?"

"Dr. Spencer, aka the guy who has you so distracted."

"I have to work with the man. Going for 'it' would only complicate our work relationship."

"His asking you out hasn't already complicated things?"

"Not really, because I haven't let it." She hadn't. She'd made a point to keep their banter light, not act any differently around him.

If she'd had to make a point, did that mean the dynamics between them had already changed?

"Meaning?"

"Meaning I don't take him seriously."

"He's looking at you as if he's serious."

There was that look. That heavenly making-her-want-to-squirm-in-her-chair look.

"Maybe."

"Definitely."

But then suddenly he wasn't looking at her.

He'd rushed over to one of the dinner tables and wrapped his arms around a rather rosy-faced gentleman who was grabbing at his throat. Everyone at the man's table was on their feet, but looking lost as to what to do.

McKenzie's natural instincts kicked in. She grabbed her purse and phone. Calling 911 as she did so, she rushed over to where Lance gave the man a hearty thrust. Nothing happened. The guy's eyes bulged out, more from fear than whatever was lodged in his throat. The woman next to him was going into hysterics. The carolers had stopped singing and every eye was on what Lance was doing, trying to figure out what was going on, then gasping in shock when they realized someone was choking.

Over the phone, McKenzie requested an ambulance. Not that there was time to wait for the paramedics. There wasn't. They had to get out whatever was in the man's throat.

Lance tried repeatedly and with great force to dislodge whatever was blocking the panicking guy's airway. McKenzie imagined several ribs had already cracked at the intensity of his chest thrusts.

If the man's airway wasn't cleared, and fast, a few broken ribs weren't going to matter. He had already started turning blue and any moment was going to lose consciousness.

"We're going to have to open his airway." Lance said what she'd been thinking. *And pray they were able to establish a patent airway.*

She glanced down at the table, found the sharpest-appearing knife, and frowned at the serrated edges. She'd have made do if that had been her only option, but in her purse, on her key chain, she had a small Swiss army knife that had been a gift many years before from her grandfather. The blade was razor sharp and much more suitable for making a neat cut into someone's neck to create an artificial airway than this steak knife. She dumped the contents of her purse onto the table, grabbed her key chain and a ballpoint pen.

As the man lost consciousness, Lance continued to try to dislodge the stuck food. McKenzie disassembled the pen, removed the ink cartridge, and blew into the now empty plastic tube to clear anything that might be in the casing.

Lance eased the man down onto the floor.

"Does he still have a heartbeat?" she asked, kneeling next to where the man now lay.

"Regardless of whether or not he does, I'm going to see if CPR will dislodge the food before we cut."

Sometimes once a choking victim lost consciousness, their throat muscles relaxed enough that whatever was stuck would loosen and pop out during the force exerted to the chest during CPR. It was worth a try.

Unfortunately, chest compressions didn't work either. Time was of the essence. Typically, there was a small window of about four minutes to get oxygen inside the man's body or there would likely be permanent brain damage. If they could revive him at all.

McKenzie tilted the man's head back. When several seconds of CPR didn't give the reassuring gasp of air to let them know the food had dislodged, she flashed her crude cricothyroidotomy instruments at Lance.

"Let me do it," he suggested.

She didn't waste time responding, just felt for the indentation between the unconscious man's Adam's apple and the cricoid cartilage. She made a horizontal half-inch incision that was about the same depth into the dip. Several horrified cries and all out sobbing were going on around her, but she drowned everything out except what she was doing to attempt to save the man's life.

Once she had her incision, she pinched the flesh, trying to get the tissue to gape open. Unfortunately, the gentleman was a fleshy fellow and she wasn't satisfied with what she saw. She stuck her finger into the cut she'd made to open the area.

Once she had the opening patent, she stuck the ballpoint-pen tube into the cut to maintain the airway and gave two quick breaths.

"Good job," Lance praised when the man's chest rose and fell. "He still has a heartbeat."

That was good news and meant their odds of reviving him were greatly improved now that he was getting oxygen again. She waited five seconds, then gave another breath, then another until their patient slowly began coming to.

"It's okay," Lance reassured him, trying to keep the man calm, while McKenzie gave one last breath before straightening from her patient.

"Dr. Sanders opened your airway," Lance continued. "Paramedics are on their way. You're going to be okay."

Having regained consciousness, the man should resume breathing on his own through the airway she'd created for him. She watched for the reassuring rise and fall of his chest. Relief washed over her at his body's movement.

Looking panicky, he sat up. Lance held on to him to help steady him and grabbed the man's hands when he reached for the pen barrel stuck in his throat.

"I wouldn't do that," Lance warned. "That's what's letting air into your body. Pull it out, and we'll have to put it back in to keep that airway open."

"Is he going to be okay?" a well-dressed, well-made-up woman in her mid-to-late fifties asked, kneeling next to McKenzie a little shakily.

"He should be." She met the scared man's gaze. "But whatever is stuck in your throat is still there. An ambulance is on the way. They'll take you to the hospital where a general surgeon will figure out the best way to remove whatever is trapped there."

The man looked dazed. He touched a steady trickle of blood that was running down his neck.

"Once the surgeon reestablishes your airway, he'll close you up and that will only leave a tiny scar," she assured him.

Seeming to calm somewhat the longer he was conscious, the man's gaze dropped to her bloody finger. Yeah, she should probably wash that off now that the immediate danger had passed.

"Go wash up," Lance ordered, having apparently read her mind. "I'll stay with him until the ambulance arrives."

With one last glance at her patient she nodded, stood, and went in search of a ladies' room so she could wash the blood off her hands and her Swiss army knife.

Carrying McKenzie's purse and the contents she'd apparently gathered up, Cecilia fell into step beside her. "Omigosh. I can't believe that just happened. You were amazing."

McKenzie glanced at her gushing friend. "Not exactly the festive cheer you want spread at a charity Christmas show."

"You and Dr. Spencer were wonderful," Cecilia sighed.

She shrugged. "We just did our job."

"Y'all weren't at work." Cecilia held the bathroom door open for McKenzie.

"Doesn't mean we'd let someone choke to death right in front of us."

"I know that, I just meant..." Cecilia paused as they went into the bathroom. She flipped the water faucet on full blast so McKenzie wouldn't have to touch the knobs with her bloodstained hands.

"It was no big deal. Really." McKenzie scrubbed the blood from her finger and from where it had smeared onto her hands. Over and over with a generous amount of antibacterial soap she scrubbed her skin and then cleaned her knife. She'd rub alcohol on it later that evening, too. Maybe even run it through the autoclave machine at work for good measure.

Cecilia talked a mile a minute, going on and on about how she'd thought she was going to pass out when McKenzie had cut the man's throat. "I could never do your job," she added.

"Yeah, and no one would want me to do yours. They'd look like a two-year-old got hold of them with kitchen shears."

When she finally felt clean, she and Cecilia returned to the dinner theater to see the paramedics talking to the man who'd choked. Although he couldn't verbalize, the man nodded or shook his head in response.

As he was doing well since his oxygenation had returned to normal, they had him climb onto the stretcher and they rolled him out of the large room. Lance followed, giving one of the guys a full report of what had happened. McKenzie fell into step with them.

"Dr. Sanders saved his life," Lance told them.

He would have established an airway just as easily as she had. It wasn't that big a deal.

The paramedic praised her efforts.

She shook off the compliment. It's what she'd trained for.

"You're going to need to go to the hospital, too," Lance reminded her.

Her gaze cut to his, then she frowned. Yeah, she'd

thought of that as she'd been scrubbing the blood from the finger she'd used to open the cut she'd made. Blood exposure was a big deal. A scary big deal.

"I know. I rode here with Cecilia. I'll have her take me, unless I can hitch a ride with you guys." She gave the paramedic a hopeful look.

"I'll take you," Lance piped up, which was exactly what she hadn't wanted to happen. The less she was alone with him the better.

She arched a brow at him. "You got blood on you, too?"

He didn't answer, just turned his attention to the paramedic. "I'll bring her to the hospital and we'll draw necessary labs."

In the heat of the moment she'd have done exactly the same thing and saved the man's life. After the fact was when one started thinking about possible consequences of blood exposure. In an emergency situation one did what one had to do to preserve another's life.

She didn't regret a thing, because she'd done the right thing, but her own life could have just drastically changed forever, pending on the man's health history.

She didn't have any cuts or nicks that she could see on her hands, but even the tiniest little micro-tear could be a site for disease to gain entry into her body.

Whether she wanted to or not, she had to have blood tests.

"Cecilia can take me," she assured Lance. Beyond being alone with him, the last thing she wanted was to have to have him there when she had labs drawn.

McKenzie hated having blood drawn.

Blood didn't bother her, so long as it was someone else's blood. Really, it wasn't her blood that was the problem. It was her irrational fear of needles that bothered her. The thought of a needle coming anywhere near her body did funny things to her mind. Like send her into a full-blown panic attack. How could she be so calm and collected when she was the one wielding the needle and so absolutely terrified when she was going to be the recipient?

She could do without Lance witnessing her belonephobia. He didn't need to know she was afraid of needles. Uh-uh, no way.

McKenzie gave Cecilia a pleading look, begging for her friend to somehow rescue her, but the grinning hairdresser hugged her goodbye and indicated that she was going to say something to someone she knew, then headed out rather than stay for the remainder of the show. Unfortunately, several of the other attendees seemed to be making the same decision to leave.

"I'm going to the hospital anyway, so it wouldn't make sense for someone else to bring you."

"But I…" She realized she was being ridiculous. One of the local doctors going into hysterics over getting a routine phlebotomy check would likely cause a stir of gossip. Lance would end up hearing about her silliness anyway. "Okay, that's fine, but don't you have to finish your show?"

He glanced back toward the dinner theater. "Other than thanking everyone for coming to the show, I've done my part. While you were washing up, I asked one of the singers to take over. The show can go on without me." A worried look settled on his handsome face. "The show must go on. It's for such a great cause and I don't want what happened to give people a bad view of the event. It's one of our biggest fund-raisers."

McKenzie frowned, hating that the incident had happened for many reasons. "It's not the fault of Celebrate Graduation that the man choked. Surely people understand that."

"You'd think so," he agreed, as they exited the building and headed toward the parking lot. "That man was Coopersville's mayor, you know."

"The mayor?" No, she hadn't known. Not that it would have mattered. She'd done what had needed to be done and would have done exactly the same regardless of who the person had been. A life had been on the line.

"Yep, Leo Jones."

"Is he one of your patients?" she asked, despite knowing he shouldn't answer. He knew exactly why she was asking. Did she need to worry about the man's health history? Did Lance know anything that would set her mind at ease?

"You know I wouldn't tell you even if he was."

Yes, she knew.

"But I can honestly say I know nothing about any mayor's health history." He opened the passenger door to his low-slung sports car that any other time McKenzie would have whistled in appreciation of. Right now her brain was distracted by too many possibilities of the consequences of her actions and that soon a needle would be puncturing her skin.

Was it her imagination or had she just broken a sweat despite the mid-December temperatures?

"Thank you," she whispered back, knowing her question had put him in an awkward position and that he'd answered as best he could. "I guess I won't know anything for a few days."

"Probably not." He stood at the car door for a few seconds. A guilty look on his face, he raked his fingers through his hair. "I should have cut the airway, rather than let you do it."

She frowned at him. "Why?"

"Because then you wouldn't be worrying about any of this."

She shrugged. "It was my choice to make."

"I shouldn't have let you."

"You think you could have stopped me from saving his life?"

His grip tightening on the car door, he shook his head. "That's not what I meant."

"I know what you meant and I appreciate the sentiment, but I'm not some froufrou girl who needs pampering. I knew the risks and I took them." She stared straight into his eyes, making sure he didn't misunderstand. "If there are consequences, I'll face them. I did the right thing."

"Agreed, except I should have been the one who took the risks."

"Because you're a guy?"

He seemed to consider her question a moment, then shook his head. "No, because you're you and I don't want anything bad to happen to you."

His answer rang with so much sincerity that, heart pounding, she found herself staring up at him. "You'd rather it happen to you?"

"Absolutely."

CHAPTER TWO

LANCE DROVE TO the hospital in silence. Just as well. McKenzie didn't seem to be in the mood to talk.

Was she thinking about what he'd said? Or the events of the evening? Of the risks she'd taken?

When he'd realized Leo Jones had been choking, he'd rushed to the man and performed the Heimlich maneuver. Too bad he hadn't been successful. Then McKenzie wouldn't have any worries about blood exposure.

Why hadn't he insisted on performing the procedure to open Leo's airway? He should have. He'd offered, but precious time had been wasting that could have meant the difference between life and death, between permanent brain damage and no complications.

He'd let her do what she'd competently done with quick and efficient movements. She'd saved the man's life. But Lance would much rather it was him being the one worrying about what he'd been exposed to.

Why? Was she right? Was it because she was female and he was male and that automatically made him feel protective?

Most likely he'd feel he should have been the one to take the risks regardless of whether McKenzie had been male or female. But the fact she was female did raise the guilt factor, with the past coming back to haunt him that he'd failed to protect another woman once upon a time when he should have.

Plus, he'd been the one to invite McKenzie to the show. If he hadn't done so she wouldn't have been at the community center, wouldn't have been there to perform the cricothyroidotomy, wouldn't have possibly been exposed to something life threatening.

Because of him, she'd taken risks she shouldn't have had to take. Guilt gutted him.

If he could go back in time, he'd undo that particular invitation. If he could go back in time, he'd undo a lot of things.

Truthfully, he hadn't expected McKenzie to accept his invitation to watch his show. She'd shot down all his previous ones with polite but absolute refusals.

He glanced at where she stared out the window from the passenger seat. Why had she semiaccepted tonight?

Perhaps the thought of seeing him onstage had been irresistible. He doubted it. She'd only agreed to go and watch and so had technically not been there as his date.

Regardless, he'd been ecstatic she'd said she'd be there. Why it mattered so much, he wasn't sure. Just that knowing McKenzie had been attending the show had really upped the ante.

Not knowing if she'd let him or not, he reached out, took her hand, and gave a squeeze meant to reassure.

She didn't pull away, just glanced toward him in question.

"It's going to be okay." He hoped he told the truth.

"I know. It's not that."

"Then what?"

She shook her head.

"Seriously, you can tell me. I'll understand. I've had blood exposure before. I know it's scary stuff until you're given the all-clear."

She didn't look at him, just stared back out the window. "I don't want to talk about it."

"What do you want to talk about?"

She glanced toward him again. "With you?"

He made a pretense of looking around the car. "It would seem I'm your only option at the moment."

"I'd rather not talk at all.

"Ouch."

"Sorry." She gave a nervous sigh. "I'm not trying to be rude. I just…"

"You just…?" he prompted at her pause.

"Don't like needles." Her words were so low, so torn from her that he wasn't sure he'd heard her correctly.

Her answer struck him as a little odd considering she was a highly skilled physician who'd just expertly performed a procedure to open a choking man's airway.

When he didn't immediately respond, she jerked her hand free from his, almost as if she'd been unaware until that moment that he even held her hand.

"Don't judge me."

How upset she was seemed out of character with everything he knew about her. She was always calm, cool, collected. Even in the face of an emergency she didn't lose her cool. Yet she wasn't calm, cool or collected at the moment. "Who's judging? I didn't say a word."

"You didn't have to."

"Maybe I'm not the one judging?"

She didn't answer.

"If you took my moment of silence in the wrong way, I'm sorry. I was just processing that you didn't like needles and that it seemed a little odd considering your profession."

"I know."

"Yet you're ultrasensitive about it."

"It's not something I'm proud of."

Ah, he was starting to catch on. McKenzie didn't like

to have a weakness, to be vulnerable in regard to anything. That he understood all too well and had erected some major protective barriers years ago to keep himself sane. Then again, he deserved every moment of guilt he experienced and then some.

"Lots of people have a fear of needles," he assured her. They saw it almost daily at the clinic.

"I passed out the last time I had blood drawn." Her voice was condemning of herself.

"Happens to lots of folks."

"I had to take an antianxiety medication to calm a panic attack before I could even make myself sit in the phlebotomist's chair and then I still passed out."

"Not unheard of."

"But not good for a doctor to be that way when she goes around ordering labs for her patients. What kind of example do I set?"

"People have different phobias, McKenzie. You can't help what you're afraid of. It's not like we get to pick and choose."

She seemed to consider what he'd said.

"What are your phobias, Lance?"

Her question caught him off guard. He wasn't sure he had any true phobias. Sure, there were things that scared him, but none that put him into shutdown mode.

Other than memories of Shelby and his immense sense of failure where she was concerned.

Could grief and regret be classified as a phobia? Could guilt?

"Death," he answered, although it wasn't exactly the full truth.

She turned to face him. "Death?"

His issues came more from having been left behind when someone he'd loved had died.

When his high school sweetheart had died.

When it should have been him and not her who'd lost their life that horrific night.

When he didn't answer, she turned in her seat. "You are, aren't you? You're afraid of dying."

Better she think that than to know the horrible truth. He shrugged. "Aren't most people, to some degree? Regardless, it isn't anything that keeps me awake at night."

Not every night as it had those first few months, at any rate. He'd had to come to terms with the fact that he couldn't change what had happened, no matter how much he wanted to, no matter how many times people told him it wasn't his fault. Now he lived his life to help others, as Shelby would have had she lived, and prevent others from making the same mistakes two teenagers had on graduation night.

"The thought of needles doesn't keep me awake at night," McKenzie said, drawing him back to the present. "Just freaks me out at the thought of a needle plunging beneath my skin."

Again, her response seemed so incongruent with her day-to-day life. She was a great physician, performed lots of in-office procedures that required breaking through the skin.

"Is there something in your past that prompted your fear?" he asked, to keep his thoughts away from his own issues. Shelby haunted him enough already.

From the corner of his eye as he pulled into the hospital physician parking area he saw her shake her head.

"Not that I recall. I've just always been afraid of needles."

Her voice quivered a little and he wondered if she told the full truth.

"Medical school didn't get you over that fear?"

"Needles only bother me when they are pointed in my direction."

"You can dish them out but not take them, eh?"

"I get my influenza vaccination annually and I'm up to date on all my other immunizations, thank you very much."

He laughed at her defensive tone. "I was only teasing you, McKenzie."

"If you knew how stressful getting my annual influenza vaccination is for me, you wouldn't tease me." She sighed. "This is the one thing I don't take a joke about so well."

"Only this?" he asked as he parked the car and turned off the ignition.

Picking up her strappy purse, she shrugged. "I'm not telling you any more of my secrets, Lance."

"Afraid to let me know your weaknesses?" he taunted.

"What weaknesses?" she countered, causing him to chuckle.

That was one of the things that attracted him to McKenzie. She made him laugh and smile.

They got out of the car and headed into the hospital.

The closer they got to the emergency department, the more her steps slowed. So much so that currently she appeared to be walking through molasses.

"You okay?"

"Fine." Her answer was more gulped than spoken.

Stupid question on his part. He could tell she wasn't. Her face was pale and she looked like she might be ill. She'd made light of her phobia, but it was all too real.

Protectiveness washed over him and he wanted to scoop her up and carry her the rest of the way.

"I'll stay with you while you have your labs drawn."

Not meeting his eyes, she shook her head. "I don't want you to see me like that."

"You think I'm going to think less of you because you're afraid of needles?"

"I fully expect you to tease me mercilessly now that you know this."

Her voice almost broke and he fought his growing urge to wrap her up into his arms. If only he could.

"You're wrong, McKenzie. I don't want to make light of anything that truly bothers you. I want to make it all better, to make this as easy for you as possible. Let me."

"Fine." She gave in but didn't sound happy about it. "Write an order for blood exposure labs. Get the emergency room physician to get consent, then draw blood on our dear mayor. Let's hope he's free from all blood-borne pathogens."

He definitely hoped that. If McKenzie came to any harm due to having done the cricothyroidotomy he'd never forgive himself for not insisting on doing the procedure, for putting her in harm's way. He'd not protected one woman too many already in his lifetime.

McKenzie counted to ten. Then she counted backward. Next she counted in her very limited Spanish retained from two years of required high school classes. She closed her eyes and thought of happy thoughts. She told her shoulders to relax, her heart not to burst free from her chest, her breath not to come in rapid pants, her blood not to jump around all quivery-like in her vessels.

None of her distraction techniques worked.

Her shoulders and neck had tight knots. Her heart pounded so hard she thought it truly might break free from her rib cage. Her breathing was labored. Her blood jumped and quivered.

Any moment she half expected her feet to take on minds of their own and to run from the lab where she waited for the phlebotomist to draw her blood.

Lance sat with her, telling her about Mr. Jones and that the surgeon was currently with him. "Looks like they're taking him into surgery tonight to remove the stuck food and close the airway opening you made."

Only half processing what he said, she nodded. She tried to focus on his words, but her skin felt as if it was on fire and her ears had to strain beyond the burn.

"The surgeon praised the opening you made. He said it would be a cinch to close and would only leave a tiny scar."

Again, she nodded.

"He also said you'd nicked two main arteries and the guy was going to have to be seen by a vascular surgeon. Shame on you."

As what he said registered, her gaze cut to Lance's. "What? I didn't nick a main artery, much less two. What are you talking about?"

The corner of his mouth tugged upward. "Sorry. I could tell your mind was elsewhere. I was just trying to get your attention back onto me."

"I didn't hit two arteries," she denied again.

"No, you didn't. The surgeon really did praise you, but didn't say a thing about any nicked arteries."

"You're bad," she accused.

Not bothering to deny her claim, he just grinned. "Sometimes."

"All the time."

"Surely you don't believe that? I come with good references."

"You get references from the women you've dated?"

"I didn't say the references were from women or from previous dates. Just that I had references."

"From?"

"My mother."

She rolled her eyes and tried not to pay attention to the man who entered the room holding her lab order. He checked over her information, verifying all the pertinent details.

Her heartbeat began to roar in her ears at a deafening level.

"You should meet her sometime," Lance continued as if she weren't on the verge of a major come-apart.

"Nice penguin suit, Dr. Spencer," the phlebotomist teased, his gaze running over Lance's spiffy suit.

"Thanks, George, I'm starting a new trend."

"Pretty sharp-looking, but good luck with that," the phlebotomist said, then introduced himself to McKenzie. "In case you didn't catch it, I'm George."

He then verified her name and information, despite the fact McKenzie had seen him around the hospital in the past. She imagined he had a checklist he had to perform.

So did she. Sit in this chair. Remain calm. Do not pass out. Do not decide to forget the first three items on her checklist and run away as fast as she could.

She clenched and unclenched her sweaty hands.

"She'd like you," Lance continued as if the phlebotomist hadn't interrupted their conversation about his mother and wasn't gathering his supplies.

Oh, she didn't want anyone else to know of her phobia. Why couldn't she just tell herself everything was going to be fine and then believe it? Everything was going to be fine. People did not die from having blood drawn. She knew that logically. But logic had nothing to do with what was happening inside her body.

"McKenzie?"

Her gaze lifted to Lance's.

"You should go to dinner with me sometime."

"No." She might be distracted, but she wasn't that distracted.

"You have other plans?"

"I do."

"I haven't said which day I wanted to take you to dinner. Maybe I wanted to take you out over the holidays."

"Doesn't matter. I don't want to go to dinner with you. Not now or over the holidays."

"Ouch."

"That's my line," she told him, watching George with growing dread.

The phlebotomist swiped an alcohol pad across her left antecubital space. "Relax your arm."

Yeah, right.

Lance moved closer. "McKenzie, you have to relax your arm or he can't stick you."

Exactly. That's why her arm wasn't relaxed.

Lance took her right hand and gave it a squeeze. "Look at me, McKenzie."

She did. She locked her gaze with his and forced her brain to stay focused on him rather than George. That really shouldn't have been a problem except George held the needle he was lowering toward her arm.

She wanted to pull away but she just gripped Lance's hand all the tighter.

She wanted to run, but she kept her butt pasted into her chair. Somehow.

"Keep your eyes on me, McKenzie."

Her eyes were on him, locked into a stare with him. It wasn't helping. All she could think about was George and his blasted needle.

She was going to pass out.

Lance lifted her hand to his lips and pressed a kiss to her clenched fingers.

McKenzie frowned. "What was that for?"

"You've had a rough evening."

"You shouldn't have done that."

"Sure, I should have. You deserve accolades for everything you've done."

"That's ridiculous. I just did my job."

"You're going to feel a stick," George warned, and she did.

Sweat drenched her skin.

Lance took the man's words as permission to do whatever he pleased. Apparently, kissing her hand again pleased him because he pressed another kiss to her flesh. This time his mouth lingered.

"Stop that." She would have pulled away but she was too terrified to move. Plus, her mind was going dark. "I think I'm going to pass out," she warned as the needle connected with its target.

She gritted her teeth, but didn't move. Couldn't move.

"Stay with me, McKenzie."

"No."

He laughed. "You planning to sleep through this?"

"Something like that." Her gaze dropped to where George swapped one vial for another as he drew blood from her arm.

She shouldn't have looked. She shouldn't have.

"Hey."

Lance's rough tone had her gaze darting back to him.

"Stay with me or I might have to do mouth-to-mouth."

"You wouldn't dare."

"Oh, I'd dare." He waggled his brows. "Do you think I have a shot at dating you?"

"Not a chance." She glowered at him. Really? He was going to ask her that now?

"Then I should go ahead with that mouth-to-mouth while you're in a compromised situation."

"I'm not that compromised," she warned, curling her free-from-George fingers into a fist.

"Don't mind me, folks. I'm just doing my job here," George assured them with a chuckle.

"I'm doing my best not to mind you." Actually, she was doing her best not to think about him and that needle.

"You're doing fine," he praised.

Amazingly, she was doing better than she'd have dreamed possible. She glanced toward Lance.

He was why she was doing better than expected. Because he was distracting her. With threats of mouth-to-mouth.

Her heart was pounding from fear, not thoughts of Lance's mouth on hers, not of him taking advantage of her compromised situation.

George removed the needle from her arm. McKenzie glanced down, saw the sharp tip, and another wave of clamminess hit her.

She lifted her gaze to Lance's to tell him she was about to go out.

"McKenzie, don't do it." He snapped his fingers in front of her face, as if that would somehow help. "Stay with me."

But out she went.

CHAPTER THREE

"GIVE IT A REST, MCKENZIE. I'm seeing you inside your place." Lance maneuvered his car into the street McKenzie had indicated he should turn at. He'd wanted to punch her address into his GPS, but she'd refused to do more than say she'd tell him where he could go.

Yeah, he had no doubt she'd do exactly that and exactly in what direction she'd point him. He suspected it would be hellish hot there, too.

She crossed her arms. "Just because I passed out, it doesn't give you permission to run roughshod over me."

"Is that what I'm doing?" He glanced toward her. Finally, her color had returned and her cheeks blushed with a rosiness that belied that she'd been as white as a ghost less than an hour before.

Her lips twisted. "Maybe."

"You have had a lot happen tonight, including losing consciousness. Of course I'm concerned and going to make sure you get inside your place, okay?"

"I think you're overreacting."

"I think you're wasting your breath trying to convince me to drop you at the curb and drive away."

"That's not what I said for you to do."

"No, but the thought of inviting me into your place scares you."

"I never said that."

"You didn't have to."

"You're imagining things. I came to your Christmas show."

"You brought a friend." As long as they were bantering she'd stay distracted, wouldn't think about having passed out.

"You were part of the show. It wasn't as if you were going to sit beside me and carry on conversation."

He shot a quick glance toward where she sat in the passenger seat with her arms crossed defensively over her chest.

"Is that what you wanted?" he asked. "For me to be at the dinner table beside you?"

"If I'd been on a date with you, that's exactly what I would have expected. Since I was just there watching your show as a friend and someone who wanted to help support a great cause, it's not a big deal."

"I could take you to a Christmas show in Atlanta, McKenzie. We could go to dinner, or to a dinner show."

"Why would you do that?"

"So I could sit beside you and carry on conversation."

"I don't want you to sit beside me and carry on conversation." She sounded like a petulant child and they both knew it. She was also as cute as all get-out and he couldn't help but smile.

"Isn't that what we're doing right now?"

"Right now you are bringing me home, where you can walk me to my front door, and then you can leave."

"What if I want to come inside?" He couldn't help but push, just to see what she'd say. He had no intention of going inside McKenzie's place, unless it was to be sure she really did make it safely inside.

Her eyes widened. "We've not even been on a date. What makes you think I'd let you stay?"

"You're jumping to conclusions, McKenzie. Just because I said I wanted to come inside, it didn't mean I planned to stay."

"Right," she huffed. She turned to stare out the window.

"Then again, I guess it's a given that I want to stay. I think you and I would have a good time."

She sighed. "Maybe."

"You don't sound enthused about the prospect."

"There is no prospect. You and I are coworkers, nothing more."

"You came to my show tonight."

"Coworkers can support one another outside work without it meaning anything."

"I see how you look at me, McKenzie."

McKenzie blinked at the man driving her home. More like driving her crazy.

How she looked at him?

"What are you talking about? You're the one who looks at me as if you've not seen a woman in years."

"I'm sure I do, but we're not talking about how I look at you. We're talking about how you look at me."

"I don't look at you."

"Yes, you do."

"How do I look at you, Lance?"

"As if you've not seen a man in years."

"That's ridiculous." She motioned for him to make a right turn.

"But nonetheless true. And now that I've had to do mouth-to-mouth to revive you, you know you're dying for another go at these lips." Eyes twinkling, he puckered up and kissed the air.

"You have such an inflated ego," she accused, glad to see him pull into her street. A few more minutes and she'd be able to escape him and this conversation she really didn't want to be having. "Besides, you did not do mouth-to-mouth. I passed out. I didn't go into respiratory arrest."

"Where you are concerned, I didn't want to take any chances, thus the mouth-to-mouth." His tone was teasing. "You were unconscious, so you probably don't recall it. George offered to help out, but I assured him I had things under control."

"Right." She rolled her eyes. She knew 100 percent he'd not taken advantage of her blacking out to perform mouth-to-mouth, even though when she'd come to he'd been leaning over her. She also knew the phlebotomist had offered to do no such thing. "Guess that's something we really do have in common, because I don't want to take any chances either. Not with the likes of you, so you'll understand that there will be no invitations into my house. Not now and not ever."

"Not ever?"

"Probably not."

McKenzie really didn't want Lance walking her to her doorway. Since she'd passed out at the hospital, she supposed she shouldn't argue as it made logical sense that he'd want to see her safely into her home. That was just a common courtesy really and didn't mean a thing if she let him. Yet the last thing she wanted was to have him on her door stoop or, even worse, inside her house.

"You have a nice place," he praised as he drove his car up into her driveway.

"It's dark. You can't really see much," she countered.

"Not so dark that I can't tell you have a well-kept yard and a nice home." As he parked the car and turned off the ignition, he chuckled. "I've never met a more prickly, stubborn woman than you, McKenzie."

She wanted to tell him to not be ridiculous, but the fact of the matter was that he was way too observant.

"I didn't ask you to be here," she reminded him defensively. She was sure she wasn't anything like the yes-women he usually spent time with. "I appreciate your concern, but I didn't ask you to drive me to the hospital or to stay with me while I had my blood drawn or to threaten me with mouth-to-mouth."

He let out an exaggerated sigh. "I'm aware you'd rather have faced George again than for me to have driven you home."

That one had her backtracking a little. "That might be taking things too far."

"Riding home with me is preferable to needles? Good to know."

He was teasing her again, but the thought she was alone with him, sitting in his car parked in her driveway, truly did make her nervous.

He made her nervous.

Memories of his lips on her hand made her nervous.

Because she'd liked the warm pressure of his mouth.

Had registered the tingly pleasure despite the way her blood had pounded from terror over what George had been up to.

At the time, she'd known Lance had kissed her as a distraction from George more than from real desire. She might have been prickly, might still be prickly, but tonight's blood draw had been one of the best she could recall, other than the whole passing-out thing. "Thank you for what you did at the emergency room."

"My pleasure."

"I didn't mean that."

"That?"

"You know."

"Do I?" He looked innocent, but they both knew he was far, far from it.

"Quit teasing me."

"But you're so much fun to tease, McKenzie." Neither of them made a move to get out of the car. "For the record, I was telling the truth."

That kissing her hand had been his pleasure?

Her face heated.

His kissing her hand had been her pleasure. She hadn't been so lost in Terrorville that she'd missed the fact that Lance had kissed her hand and it had felt good.

"I'm sorry tonight didn't go as planned for your Christmas show."

"A friend texted to let me know that they finished the show and although several left following the mayor's incident, tonight's our biggest fund-raiser yet."

"That's great."

"It is. Keeping kids off the roads on graduation night is important."

"Celebrate Graduation is a really good cause." The program was something Lance had helped get started locally after he'd moved to Coopersville four years ago. McKenzie had been away doing her residency, but she'd heard many sing his praises. "Did your school have a similar program? Is that why you're so involved?"

He shook his head. "No. My school didn't. I wish they had."

Something in his voice was off and had McKenzie turning to fully face him. Rather than give her time to ask anything further, he opened his car door and got out.

Which meant it was time for her to get out too.

Which meant she'd be going into her house.

Alone.

It wasn't a good idea to invite Lance inside her place.

She dug her keys out of her purse and unlocked her front door, then turned to him to issue words that caused an internal tug-of-war of common courtesy and survival instincts.

"Do you want to come inside?"

His gaze searched hers then, to her surprise, he shook his head. "I appreciate the offer, but I'm going to head back to the community theater to help clean up."

"Oh."

"If I didn't know better I'd think you were disappointed by my answer."

Was she?

That wasn't disappointment moving through her chest. Probably just indigestion from the stress of having to get blood drawn. Or something like that.

She lifted her chin and looked him square in the eyes. "I'm sorry I kept you from things you needed to be doing."

"I'm sure the crew has things under control, but I usually help straighten things up. Afterward, we celebrate another successful show, which I'm calling tonight despite everything that happened, because you were there and I got to spend time with you."

She glanced at her watch. "You're going out?"

"To an after-show party at Lanette and Roger Anderson's place. Lanette is one of the female singers and who I asked to take over emceeing for me." He mentioned a couple of the songs she'd done that night and a pretty brunette with an amazing set of pipes came to mind.

"She will have their place all decked out with Christmas decorations and will have made lots of food," he continued. "You want to come with me?"

She immediately shook her head. "No, thanks. I ate at the dinner show."

He laughed. "I thought you'd say no."

"You should have said you had somewhere you needed to be."

"And keep you from sweating over whether or not you were going to invite me in? Why would I do that?"

"Because you're a decent human being?"

"I am a decent human being. I have references, remember?"

"Mothers don't count."

"Mothers count the most," he corrected.

When had he moved so close? Why wasn't she backing away from him? Any moment now she expected him to close the distance between their mouths. He was that close. So close that if she stretched up on her tippy-toes her lips would collide with his.

She didn't stretch.

Neither did he close the distance between their mouths. Instead, he cupped her jaw and traced over her chin with his thumb. "You could easily convince me to change my plans."

His breath was warm against her face.

"Why would I want to do that?" But her gaze was on his mouth, so maybe her question was a rhetorical one.

He laughed and again she felt the pull of his body.

"You should give me a chance to make this up to you by taking you to the hospital Christmas party next weekend."

"I can take myself."

"You can, but you shouldn't have to."

"To think I need a man to do things for me would be a mistake. I started wearing my big-girl panties a long time ago."

His eyes twinkled. "Prove it."

"You wish."

"Without a doubt."

Yet he hadn't attempted to kiss her, hadn't taken up her offer to come inside her place where he could have attempted to persuade her into something physical. Instead, he'd said she could convince him to change his plans. He'd given her control, left the power in her hands about what happened next.

"I'll see you bright and early Monday morning, Mc-Kenzie."

"Have fun at your party."

"You could go with me and have fun, too."

She shook her head. "I wouldn't want to cramp your style."

His brows made a V. "My style?"

"What if you met someone you wanted to take home with you?"

"I already have met someone I want to take home with me. She keeps telling me no."

"I'm not talking about me."

"I am talking about you."

Exasperation filled her. She wasn't sure if it was from his insistence that he wanted her or the fact that he hadn't kissed her. Maybe both. "Would you please be serious?"

His thumb slid across her cheek in a slow caress. "Make no mistake, McKenzie. I am serious when I say that I'd like to explore the chemistry between us."

Shivers that had nothing to do with the December weather goose-pimpled her body.

"Why should I take you seriously?" she challenged. "We've been standing on my porch for five minutes and you haven't threatened mouth-to-mouth again. Much less actually made a move. I don't know what to think where you're concerned."

That's when he did what she'd thought he would do all along. It had taken her throwing down a gauntlet of challenge to prompt him into action. Lance bent just enough to close the gap between their mouths.

The pressure of his lips was gentle, warm, electric and made time stand still.

Her breath caught and yet he made her pant with want for more. She went to deepen the kiss, to search his lips for answers as to why he made her nervous, why he made her feel so alive, why he made her want to run and stay put at the same time. She closed her eyes and relaxed against the hard length of his body. He felt good. Her hands went to his shoulders, his broad shoulders that her fingers wanted to dig into.

"Good night, McKenzie," he whispered against her lips, making her eyes pop open.

"Unless you text or call saying you want to see me before then, I'll see you bright and early Monday morning. Good luck with your run tomorrow." With that he stepped back, stared into her eyes for a few brief seconds then headed toward his car.

"I wouldn't hold my breath if I were you," she called from where she stood on the porch.

He just laughed. "Thank you for my mouth-to-mouth, McKenzie. I've never felt more alive. Sweet dreams."

"You're not welcome," she muttered under her breath while he got into his car, then had the audacity to wave goodbye before pulling out of her driveway. Blasted man.

McKenzie's dreams weren't sweet.

They were filled with hot, sweaty, passionate kisses.

So much so that when she woke, glanced at her phone and saw that it was only a little after midnight, she wanted to scream in protest. She'd been asleep for less than an hour. Ugh.

She should text him to tell him to get out of her dreams and to stay out. She didn't want him there.

Wouldn't he get a kick out of that?

Instead, she closed her eyes and prayed.

Please go back to sleep.

Please don't dream of Lance.

Please no more visions of Lance kissing me and me begging for so much more instead of watching him drive away.

Please don't let me beg a man for anything. I don't want to be like my mother.

I won't be like my mother.

CHAPTER FOUR

EDITH WINTERS CAME into the clinic at least once a month, always with a new chief complaint. Although she had all the usual aging complaints that were all too real, most of the time McKenzie thought the eighty-year-old was lonely and came in to be around other humans who cared about her.

The woman lived alone, had no local family, and her only relative as far as McKenzie knew was a son who lived in Florida and rarely came home to visit.

"How long have these symptoms been bothering you, Mrs. Winters?"

"Since last week."

Last week. Because when you had severe abdominal pain and no bowel movements for four days it was normal to wait a week to seek care. Not.

"I didn't want to bother anyone."

"Any time a symptom is severe and persistent, you need to be checked further."

"I would have come sooner if I'd gotten worse."

Seriously, she'd seen Edith less than a month ago and it had only been two weeks prior to that she'd been in the clinic for medication refills. Severe abdominal pain and no bowel movement was a lot more than what usually prompted her to come to the clinic. "What made you decide you needed to be seen?"

The woman had called and, although McKenzie's schedule had been full, she'd agreed for the woman to be checked. She'd grown quite fond of the little lady and figured she'd be prescribing a hug and reassurance that everything was fine.

"There was blood when I spit up this morning."

McKenzie's gaze lifted from her laptop. "What do you mean, when you spat up?"

Her nurse had said nothing about spitting up blood.

"It wasn't really a throw-up, but I heaved and there was bright red blood mixed in with the stuff that came up."

Bright red blood. Abdominal pain the woman described as severe.

"Have you ever had an ulcer?"

Edith shook her head. "Not that I know of, but my memory isn't what it used to be."

"I'm going to get some labs on you and will decide from there what our next best step is. I may need to admit you, at least overnight, to see what's up with that bright red blood."

Speaking of labs, she needed to log in and see if her labs from the other night were available online. George had told her they should show up on Monday. She should be notified of the mayor's results today, too.

Although there would still be some risks involved, once she had the mayor's negative ones, she'd breathe much easier. Assuming the mayor's results were negative.

She prayed they would be.

She hadn't allowed herself much downtime to consider the ramifications of her actions. How could she when she'd been so distracted by a certain doctor's kiss? But this morning when she'd run she'd not been able to keep the pending results out of her head. She'd run and run and hadn't wanted to stop when she'd had to turn back or she'd have been late into work.

McKenzie examined the frail little woman in her examination room, then filled out the lab slip. "I'll see you back after your blood is drawn."

She left the room, gave the order to her nurse, then went into the examination room.

An hour later, she was heading toward her office when her cell phone rang. She glanced at the screen and recognized the hospital's number. She stopped walking.

"Dr. Sanders," she answered.

"Hi, Dr. Sanders. This is Melissa from the lab. The ER doc looked over your results and wanted to let you know that all of your labs came back negative, as did those of the subject whose blood you were exposed to. He thought you'd want to know ASAP."

Almost leaning against the clinic hallway wall, she let out a sigh of relief. "He's right and that's great news."

"You know the drill, that you and the person you were exposed to will both need to have routine repeat labs per protocol?"

She knew. She finished the call then clicked off the phone, barely suppressing the urge to jump up and yell, "Yes!"

"Your labs were good?"

She jumped at Lance's voice. She hadn't heard him come up behind her in the hallway.

"Don't do that," she ordered, frowning. Mostly she frowned to keep her face preoccupied because instantly, on looking at him, she had a flashback to the last time she'd seen him.

On her front porch when he'd kissed her and completely rewired her circuitry.

That had to be it because she didn't fantasize about men or kisses or things way beyond kisses, yet that's exactly what she'd done more often than she'd like to admit since Friday night.

"Sorry." He studied her a little too closely for her liking. "I didn't realize I'd startle you or I would have made some noise when walking up."

She stepped into her office and he followed, stomping his feet with each step.

She rolled her eyes.

"So your tests are all negative?"

She nodded without looking at him because looking at him did funny things to her insides.

"Thank goodness." He sounded as relieved as she'd felt. "The mayor's too?"

She nodded again.

"That is great news."

She set her laptop down on her desk then faced him. "Was there something you needed?"

He shook his head. "I was checking to see if you'd heard anything on your labs."

She waved the phone she still held. "Perfect timing."

He waggled his brows. "We should go celebrate."

Not bothering to hide her surprise, she eyed him. "Why?"

"Because you got great news that deserves celebrating."

She needed to look away from those baby blues, needed to not think about his amazing smile that dug dimples into his cheeks, needed to not stare at his magical lips that had put her under some kind of spell.

"My great news doesn't involve you," she reminded him, not doing any of the things she'd just told herself to do.

"Sure it does. I was there, remember?"

How could she ever forget? Which was the problem. So much about that night plagued her mind. Lance acting so protective of her as he'd driven her to the hospital and stayed during her blood draw. Lance taking her home. Lance kissing her.

Lance. Lance. Lance.

Yeah, he had definitely put her under a spell. Under his kiss.

Her cheeks heated at the memory and she hoped he couldn't read her mind. Her gaze met his and, Lord, she'd swear he could, that he knew exactly where her thoughts were.

Don't think of that kiss. Don't think of that kiss. Just don't think at all.

"My news doesn't involve you," she repeated, reminding herself that she worked with him. She wasn't like her father who'd drag any willing member of the opposite sex into his office for who knew what? A relationship with Lance would be nothing short of disastrous in the long run.

Plus, there was how she couldn't get him out of her head. What kind of stupid would she be if she risked getting further involved with someone who made her react so differently from how she did to every other man she'd met? To do so would be like playing Russian roulette with the bullet being to end up like her mother. She was her own person, nothing like her parents.

"You're a stubborn woman, McKenzie." He sounded as if that amused him more than upset him.

"You're a persistent man, Lance," she drily retorted, trying to look busy so he'd take the hint and leave. She wanted out from under those eagle eyes that seemed to see right through her.

Instead, he sat on the desk corner and laughed. "Just imagine what we could accomplish if we were on the same team."

"We aren't enemies." Maybe that was how she should regard him after that treacherous and oh-so-unforgettable kiss.

His gaze held hers and sparked with something so intense McKenzie struggled to keep her breathing even.

"But you aren't willing to be more than my friend."

She wasn't sure if he was making a comment or asking a question. Her gaze fell to her desk and she stared at a durable medical equipment request form she needed to sign for a patient's portable oxygen tanks. Her insides shook and her vision blurred, making reading the form impossible. They did need to just be friends. And coworkers. Not lovers.

"I didn't say that." McKenzie's mouth fell open. What had she just said? She hadn't meant to say anything and certainly not something that implied she'd be willing to share another kiss with him.

She wouldn't, would she?

"You are willing?" He asked what was pounding through her head.

"I didn't say that either." She winced. Poor man. She was probably confusing the heck out of him because she was confusing herself.

Despite her wishy-washiness, he didn't seem upset. Actually, he smiled as if he thought she was the greatest thing since sliced bread. "You want to go get frozen yogurt tonight?"

Totally caught off guard by his specific request, she blinked. "Frozen yogurt? With you?"

Was he nuts? It was December and thirty or so degrees outside. They were having a serious conversation about their relationship and he'd invited her to go get frozen yogurt? Really? That was his idea of celebrating her good news?

Why was she suddenly craving the cold dessert?

"They're donating twenty percent of their take to the Sherriff's Toys for Tots fund tonight. We could sit, eat frozen yogurt. You could tell me about your half marathon on Saturday morning. I heard you won your age division."

Oh.

"You wouldn't say no to helping give kids toys for Christmas, would you?"

No, she wouldn't do that. "You should have gone into sales. Did I mention earlier that you were persistent?"

"Did I mention how stubborn you were?"

A smile played on her lips, then she admitted the truth. "I'll be here until late, Lance. You should go without me, but I can swing by and pick up some frozen yogurt on my way home. That way the kids can get their Christmas toys."

His grin widened, his dimples digging in deep. "You think I won't be here until late?"

"I don't know what you have going on," she admitted. She always made a point to not know what Lance was up to. She hadn't wanted to think about him, hadn't wanted to let his handsome smile and charm get beneath her skin. So much for that. She could barely think of anything else.

"We should correct that."

No, they shouldn't.

"Plus, I plan to go to the hospital to check on a patient." Edith's blood count had come back low enough that McKenzie really was concerned about a gastrointestinal bleed. Hopefully, the gastroenterologist would see her soon. Although she could pull up test results and such remotely from her office, she wanted to put eyes on her patient.

"We could ride to the hospital together, then go get frozen yogurt afterward."

They could, but should they?

"It might cause people to ask questions if we were seen at the hospital together so close on the tails of Saturday night."

"You think my kissing your hand in the lab hasn't caused a few tongues to wag?"

His kissing her hand had caused her tongue to wag when she'd returned his kiss on her front porch.

A sweet kiss that hadn't lasted nearly long enough.

A passionate kiss that had made her want to wind her

arms around him, pull him as close to her as she possibly could and kiss him until she'd had her fill.

"We're already the top story around the hospital. George has told everyone how I saved your life with mouth-to-mouth when you passed out."

Heat flushed her face. "You did not do mouth-to-mouth on me in the lab."

He arched a brow. "You sure? You are still alive."

Very alive. Intensely alive. Feeling more alive by the second beneath his gaze.

"You owe me." His eyes locked with hers. "Say yes."

Needing to break the contact, she rolled her eyes. "I don't owe you."

He let out an exaggerated sigh. "You're right. I'm the one who owes you. Let me make it up to you by taking you out for frozen yogurt."

Her brows made a V. "What do you owe me for?"

"That kiss."

Her cheeks flushed hot and she stared at the durable medical equipment form again, still not able to focus on it. "You don't owe me."

"Sure I do."

"Why?" She refused to glance up at him.

"Because it was an amazing kiss."

It had been an amazing kiss.

"If you said yes to going with me for frozen yogurt, I could repay you."

"With another kiss?"

"Well, I had frozen yogurt in mind, but I like how you think a lot better."

When she didn't immediately answer, he sat down on the edge of her desk and grinned down at her. "But I'm a compromising kind of guy. If you ask nicely, we could do both frozen yogurt and mouth-to-mouth."

McKenzie bit her lower lip. She wanted to say yes.

Way more than she should.

It was only frozen yogurt.

And his lips against hers.

Not giving her breath but stealing hers away.

"You think threatening me with more mouth-to-mouth is going to convince me to say yes?" She made the mistake of looking directly at him.

He stared into her eyes for long moments, that intensity back, then he nodded. "I know it is."

Her eyes widened at his confidence.

"You want me as much as I want you, McKenzie. I'm not sure why you feel you need to say no or not date me, but I'm one hundred percent positive that it's not because you don't want to be with me or that you didn't enjoy that kiss as much as I did."

"That's cocky of you."

"Honesty isn't cockiness."

"Why should I want to be with you?"

He frowned. "We get along well at the clinic and hospital. You make me smile and I make you smile. We have a lot in common, including that neither of us is looking for a long-term relationship," he pointed out. "I'm basically a nice guy."

"Who I work with," she reminded.

"That's really your hang-up? That we work together?"

Sinking her teeth into her lower lip again, McKenzie nodded. It was, wasn't it? It wasn't because he scared her emotionally, that the way she reacted to him emotionally scared her silly, that she was afraid she'd get too attached to him and end up reminding herself of her man-needing mother?

Was fear what was really holding her back?

His gaze bored into her. "If we didn't work together, you'd go out with me? Admit that there was something between us?"

"We do work together so it's a moot point," she said, as much to herself as to him, because she wasn't chicken. She wasn't afraid to become involved with Lance. If she were, that would mean admitting she really was like her mother.

She wasn't.

"But if we didn't work together, you'd go have frozen yogurt with me tonight?"

She closed her eyes then nodded. Lord help her, she would. Probably take some more of that mouth-to-mouth, too. She squeezed her eyes tighter to try to block out the image.

See, she wasn't afraid of Lance. Her reservations were because of their jobs. She heard Lance stir, wondered if he was moving toward her, if he was going to go for more mouth-to-mouth, and, when she opened her eyes, was surprised to see that he was leaving her office.

Seriously, she'd essentially just admitted that she wanted to date him, to share kisses with him, and he was leaving? Not cool.

"Where are you going?" she asked, instantly wishing she could take her question back as she didn't want him to know it bothered her he'd been leaving. *Why had he been leaving?*

"To leave you alone. We're both adults, neither of whom wants a long-term relationship. When we'd both be going in with no long-term expectations and there's no company policy against dating, that you'd use that as your reason doesn't make sense unless the truth is that I've misread the signs that you return my attraction or you're scared. Either way doesn't work for me. Sorry I've bothered you, McKenzie."

CHAPTER FIVE

MCKENZIE BOLTED OUT of her office chair and took off after Lance. She grabbed hold of his white lab coat and pulled him back into her office.

He couldn't just leave like that.

She pushed her office door closed and leaned against it, blocking his access to leave until she was ready to let him go.

"Does that mean we aren't going to be friends anymore?" Did she sound as ridiculous as she felt? He'd asked her out. She'd turned him down. Repeatedly. He'd told her he'd leave her alone. She'd stopped him. What did that say about her?

Dear Lord, she was an emotional mess where this man was concerned. She should have let him go. Why hadn't she?

"You want to just be my friend?" His blue eyes glittered with steeliness. "I'm sorry, McKenzie, but I want more than that. After our kiss, it's going to take time before I can re-wire my brain to think of you as just a friend. We can't be 'just friends.' At least, I can't think of you that way."

"Stop this," she ordered, lifting her chin in defiance at him and the plethora of emotions assailing her. "All this because I won't go get frozen yogurt with you? This is ridiculous."

"Not just frozen yogurt, McKenzie, and you know it. I want to date you. As in you and me acknowledging and embracing the attraction between us. As in multiple episodes of mouth-to-mouth and wherever that takes us. I've been honest with you that although I'm not interested in something long term, I'm attracted to you. Isn't it time you're honest with yourself and me? Because to say our working in the same building is why you won't date me is what I find ridiculous."

"But…" She trailed off, not sure what to say. Way beyond her excuse of not wanting to date a coworker, McKenzie was forced to face some truths.

She liked Lance.

She liked seeing glimpses of him every day, seeing his smile, hearing his voice, his laughter, even when it was from a distance and had nothing to do with her. She liked catching sight of him from time to time and seeing his expression brighten when he caught sight of her. She liked the way his eyes ate her up, the way his lips curved upward. She didn't want him to avoid her or not be happy when he saw her. She didn't want to stop grabbing a meal with him at the hospital or hanging out with him at group functions. She enjoyed his quick wit, his easy smile, the way he made her feel inside, even if she'd never admitted that to herself. If he shut her out of his life, she'd miss him. She'd miss everything about him.

"You can date other women," she pointed out, wondering at how her own heart was throbbing at the very idea of seeing him with other women. Not that she hadn't in the past. But in the past she'd never kissed him. Now she had and couldn't stand the thought of his lips touching anyone else's. "You can date some other woman," she continued in spite of her green-flowing blood. "Then we could still be friends."

He shook his head. "You're wrong."

"How am I wrong?"

He bent his head and touched his lips to hers.

McKenzie's heart pounded so hard in her chest she was surprised her teeth weren't rattling. But her thoughts from moments before had her kissing him back with a possessiveness she had no right to feel.

She slid her hands up his chest and twined her arms around his neck, threading her fingers into his dark hair. She kissed him until her knees felt so weak she might sag to the floor in an ooey-gooey puddle. Then she kissed him some more because she wanted him to sag to the floor in an ooey-gooey puddle with her.

The thought that he might cut her out of his life completely gave desperation to how she clung to him.

Desperate. Yep, that was her.

When he pulled slightly away he rested his forehead against hers and stared into her eyes. "That's some mouth-to-mouth, McKenzie."

She shook her head. "Mouth-to-mouth restores one's breath. That totally just stole mine."

Why was she admitting how much he affected her?

He cupped her face in a caress. "I can't pretend that doesn't exist between us. I don't even want to try. I want you, McKenzie. I want to kiss you. Your mouth, your neck, your breasts, all of you. That's not how I think of my 'friends.'"

Fighting back visions of him kissing her all over, she sighed. "You don't play fair."

His fingers stroking across her cheek, he arched his brow. "You think not? I'm being honest. What's unfair about that?"

She let out an exasperated sigh, which had him touching his lips to hers in a soft caress.

Which had her insides doing all kinds of crazy somersaults and happy dances. Okay, so maybe she'd wanted to say yes all along, but that didn't mean everything about him wasn't a very bad idea. Just as long as she kept things simple and neither of them fell under false illusions or expectations, she'd be fine.

When he lifted his head, she looked directly into his gaze.

"I will go to the hospital with you and get frozen yogurt afterward with you, but on one condition."

"Name it."

She should ask for the moon or something just as elaborately impossible. Then again, knowing him, he'd find a way to pluck it right out of the sky and deliver on time.

"No more mouth-to-mouth at work," she told him, because the knowledge that she'd dropped to her father's level with making out at work and to her mother's level of desperation already cut deep.

He whistled softly. "Not that I don't see your point, McKenzie, but that might be easier said than done."

She stepped back, which put her flat against the door. With her chin slightly tilted upward, she crossed her arms. "That's my condition."

"Okay," he agreed, but shook his head as if baffled. "But I'm just not sure how you're going to do it."

Her momentary triumph at his *Okay* dissipated. She blinked. "Me?"

Looking as cool as ever, he nodded. "Now that you know how good I am at mouth-to-mouth, how are you going to keep from pulling me behind closed doors every chance you get for a little resuscitation?"

Yeah, there was that.

"I'll manage to restrain myself." Somehow. He was very, very good at kissing, but there was that whole self-respect thing that she just as desperately clung to. "Now leave so I can work."

And beat herself up over how she'd just proved her parents' blood ran through her veins.

McKenzie looked over Edith's test results while she waited for Lance to come to her office. Her hemoglobin and hematocrit were both decreased but not urgently so. Her abdominal and pelvic computerized tomography scan didn't show any evidence of a perforated bowel or a cancerous mass, although certainly there was evidence of Edith's constipation.

Had the woman really spit up blood? If she had, where had the blood come from? Had she just coughed too hard and had a minor bleed in her bronchus? It wasn't likely, especially as Edith had said it hadn't been like throwing up.

McKenzie had ordered the gastroenterology consult. She suspected Edith would be undergoing an endoscopy to evaluate her esophagus and stomach soon. Then again, it was possible the specialist might deem that, due to her age, she wasn't a good candidate for the procedure.

"You look mind-boggled," Lance said, knocking on her open office door before coming into the room. "Thinking about how much fun you're going to have with me tonight?"

"Not that much fun," she assured him, refusing to pander to his ego any more than she must have done earlier. "I'm trying to figure out what's going on with a patient."

"Want to talk about it?"

"Not really." At his look of disappointment, she relented. "One of my regulars came in today with a history of abdominal pain, constipation, and spitting up blood that she described as not a real throw-up, but spitting up."

"Anemic?"

"Slightly, but not enough to indicate a major bleed. She always runs borderline low, but her numbers have definitely dipped a little. I'm rechecking labs in the morning."

"Have you consulted a gastroenterologist or general surgeon?"

"The first."

"Any other symptoms?"

"If you named it, Edith would say she had it."

"Edith Winters?"

Her gaze met his in surprise. "You know her?"

"Sure. I used to see her quite a bit. She's a sweet lady."

"She has me a bit worried. It's probably nothing. Maybe she drank grape juice with breakfast and that's what she saw when she spat up. I don't know. I just feel as if I'm missing something."

"You want me to have a look at her for a second opinion?"

"Would you mind?"

"I wouldn't have offered if I minded. I'll be at the hospital with you anyway."

"Good point." She got her purse from a desk drawer, then stood. "You ready to go so we can get this over with?"

"'This' as in the hospital or the night in general?"

She met his gaze, lifted one shoulder in a semishrug. "We'll see. Oh, and if you think you're going to get away with just feeding me frozen yogurt, you're wrong. I'm not one of those 'forever dieting and watching her carbs' chicks you normally date who doesn't eat. I expect real food before frozen yogurt."

Lance grinned at the woman sitting next to him in his car. Twice in less than a week she'd been in his car when he'd begun to wonder if she was ever going to admit there was something between them.

He understood her concerns regarding them working together, but it wasn't as if they worked side by side day in and day out. More like in the same office complex and caught glimpses of each other from time to time with occasional prolonged interaction. With other women he might be concerned about a "work romance," but not with Mc-

Kenzie. She was too professional to ever let a relationship interfere with work.

Thinking back over the past few months, really from the time he'd first met her a couple years ago when she'd moved back to Coopersville after finishing her medical training, he'd been fascinated by McKenzie. But other than that he'd catch her watching him with a curious look in her eyes, she hadn't seemed interested in anything more than friendship and was obviously not in a life phase where she wanted a serious relationship.

Not that he wanted that either, but he also didn't want to become last month's flavor within a few weeks. She didn't seem interested in dating anyone longer than a month. It was almost as if she marked a calendar and when thirty days hit, she moved on to the next page of her dating life.

Although he had no plans of marriage ever, he did prefer committed relationships. Just not those where his partner expected him to march her down the aisle.

He owed Shelby that much. More. So much more. But anything beyond keeping his vow to her was beyond his reach.

Since his last breakup he definitely hadn't been interested in dating anyone except McKenzie. If he was being completely honest, he hadn't been interested in dating anyone else for quite some time.

Oddly enough, since she dated regularly and routinely, she'd repeatedly turned him down. Which, since she was obviously as attracted to him as he was her, made no sense. Unless she truly was more a stickler for not dating coworkers than he believed.

"Have you ever dated a coworker in the past?"

At his question, she turned to him. "What do you mean?"

"I was just curious as to why going on a date with me was such a big deal."

"I didn't say going on a date with you was a big deal," she immediately countered.

"My references say that going on a date with me is a very big deal."

"Yeah, well, you might need to update that reference because I'm telling you Mommy Dearest doesn't count."

He grinned at her quick comeback. He liked that about her, that she had an intelligence and wit that stimulated him. "Did you think about our kiss?"

"What?"

He grinned. He knew that one would throw her off balance. "I was just curious. Did you think about our kiss on your porch this weekend?"

"I'm not answering that." She turned and stared out the window.

Lance laughed. "You don't have to. I already know."

"I don't like how you think you know everything about me."

"I wouldn't presume to say I know everything about you by a long shot, but your face and eyes are very expressive so there's some things you don't hide well."

"Such as?"

"Your feelings about me."

"Sorry. Loathing tends to do that to a girl."

There went that quick wit again. He grinned. "Keep telling yourself that and you might convince yourself, but you're not going to convince me. I've kissed you, remember?"

"How could I forget when you keep reminding me?"

He laughed again. "I plan to keep reminding you."

"I have a good memory. No reminders needed."

"I'm sure you do, but I enjoy reminding you."

"Because?"

"You normally don't fluster easily, yet I manage to fluster you."

"You say that as if it's a good thing," she accused from the passenger seat.

Seeing the heightened color in her cheeks, hearing the pitch-change to her voice, watching the way her eyes sparked to life, he smiled. "Yes, I guess I do. You need to be flustered, and flustered good."

"Why am I blushing?"

"Because you have a dirty mind?" he suggested, shooting her a teasing look. "And you liked that I kissed you today in your office and Friday night on your porch."

"Let's change the subject. Let's talk about Edith and her bowel movements."

He burst out laughing. "You have a way with words, McKenzie."

"Let's hope they include *no*, *no* and *no* again."

"Then I just have to be sure to ask the right questions, such as, do you want me to stop kissing you, McKenzie?"

She just rolled her eyes and didn't bother giving a verbal answer.

There really wasn't any need.

They both already knew that she liked him kissing her.

CHAPTER SIX

EDITH DIDN'T LOOK much the worse for wear when Mc-Kenzie entered her hospital room. The elderly woman lay in her bed in the standard drab hospital gown beneath a white blanket and sheet that were pulled up to beneath her armpits. Her skin was still a pasty pale color that blended too well with her bed covering and had poor turgor, despite the intravenous fluids. Oxygen was being delivered via a nasal cannula. Edith's short salt-and-pepper hair was sticking up every which way about her head as if she'd been restless. Or maybe she'd just run her fingers through her hair a lot.

"Hello, Edith, how are you feeling since I last saw you at the office earlier today?"

Pushing her glasses back on her nose, the woman shrugged her frail shoulders. "About the same."

Which was a better answer than feeling worse.

"Any more blood?"

Edith shifted, rearranging pillows. "Not that I've seen."

"Are you spitting up anything?"

She shook her head in a slow motion, as if to continue to answer required too much effort. "I was coughing up some yellowish stuff, but haven't since I got to the hospital."

"Hmm, I'm going to take a look and listen to you again,

and then one of my colleagues whom you've met before will also be checking you. Dr. Spencer."

"I know him. Handsome fellow. Great smile. Happy eyes."

Lance did have happy eyes. He had a great smile, too. But she didn't want thoughts of that happy-eyed handsome man with his great smile interfering with her work, so she just gave Edith a tight smile. "That would be him."

"He your fellow?"

McKenzie's heart just about stopped.

Grateful she'd just put her stethoscope diaphragm to the woman's chest, McKenzie hesitated in answering. Was Lance her fellow? Was that what she'd agreed to earlier?

Essentially she had agreed to date him, but calling him her fellow seemed a far stretch from their earlier conversation.

She made note of the slight arrhythmia present in the woman's cardiac sounds, nothing new, just a chronic issue that sometimes flared up. Edith had a cardiologist she saw regularly. Perhaps McKenzie would consult him also. First, she'd get an EKG and cardiac enzymes, just to be on the safe side.

"Take a deep breath for me," she encouraged. Edith's lung sounds were not very strong, but really weren't any different from her usual shallow and crackly breaths. "I'm going to have to see why your chest X-ray isn't available. They did do it?"

The woman nodded. "They brought the machine here and did the X-ray with me in bed."

Interesting, as Edith could get up with assistance and had walked out of the clinic of her own free will with a nurse at her side. Plus, she'd had to go to the radiology department for the CT of her abdomen. They would have taken her by wheelchair, so why the bedside X-ray rather than doing it in Radiology?

There might be a perfectly logical reason why they'd done a portable chest X-ray instead of just doing it while she'd been there for her CT scan, McKenzie told herself.

"Is there something wrong?" Edith asked.

"You're in the hospital, so obviously everything's not right," McKenzie began. "It concerns me that you saw blood when you spat up earlier. I need to figure out where that blood came from. Your esophagus? Your stomach? Your lungs? Then there's your pain. How would you rate it currently?"

"My stomach? Maybe a two or three out of ten," Edith answered, making McKenzie question if she should have sent the woman home and just seen her back in clinic in the morning.

Maybe she'd overreacted when Edith had mentioned seeing the blood. No, that was a new complaint for the woman and McKenzie's gut instinct said more was going on here than met the eye. Edith didn't look herself. She was paler, weaker.

"Does anywhere else hurt?"

"Not really."

"Explain," she prompted, knowing how Edith could be vague.

"Nothing that's worth mentioning."

Which could mean anything with the elderly woman.

"Edith, if there's anything hurting or bothering you, I need to know so I can have everything checked out before I release you from the hospital. I want to make sure that we don't miss anything."

McKenzie listened to Edith's abdomen, then palpated it, making sure nothing was grossly abnormal that hadn't shown on Edith's CT scan.

"I'm fine." The woman patted McKenzie's hand and any moment McKenzie expected to be called *dearie*. She finished her examination and was beginning to decide she'd truly jumped the gun on the admission when Lance stepped into the room.

"Hey, beautiful. What's a classy lady like you doing in a joint like this?"

McKenzie shook her head at Lance's entrance. The man was a nut. One who had just put a big smile on Edith's pale face.

"What's a hunky dude like you doing wearing pajamas to work?"

McKenzie blinked. Never had she heard Edith talk in such a manner.

Lance laughed. "They're scrubs, not pajamas, and you and I have had this conversation in the past. Good to note your memory is intact."

"That your fancy way of saying I haven't lost my marbles?"

"Something like that." He turned to McKenzie. "I'm a little confused about why they did a portable chest X-ray rather than do that while she was in Radiology for her CT."

"I wondered that myself. I'll talk to her nurse before we leave the hospital."

"We?" Edith piped up.

Before Lance could say or reveal anything that McKenzie wasn't sure she wanted to share with the elderly woman, McKenzie cleared her throat. "I suspect Dr. Spencer will be going home at some point this evening, and I certainly plan to go home too."

After real food and frozen yogurt.

And mouth-to-mouth.

Her cheeks caught fire and she prayed Edith didn't notice because the woman wouldn't bother filtering her comments and obviously she had no qualms about teasing Lance.

"After looking over everything, I'm thinking you just needed a vacation," Lance suggested.

To McKenzie's surprise, Edith sighed. "You know it's bad when your husband's doctor says you need a vacation."

Edith's husband had been gone for a few years. He'd died about the time McKenzie had returned to Coopersville and started practicing at the clinic. Edith and her husband must have been patients of Lance's prior to his death. Had the woman changed doctors at the clinic because McKenzie hadn't known her husband and therefore she'd make no associations when seeing her?

No wonder he'd been so familiar with Edith.

"What do you think is going on, Edith?" Lance asked, removing his stethoscope from his lab coat pocket.

"I think you and my doctor are up to monkey business."

McKenzie's jaw dropped.

Lance grinned. "Monkey business, eh? Is that what practicing medicine is called these days?"

"Practicing medicine isn't the business I was talking about. You know what I meant," the older woman accused, wagging her finger at him.

"As did you when I asked what you thought was going on," Lance countered, not fazed by her good-natured fussing.

The woman sighed and seemed to lose some of her gusto. "I'm not sure. My stomach has been hurting, but I just figured it was my constipation. Then today I saw that blood when I spit up, so I wasn't sure what was going on and thought I'd better let Dr. Sanders check me."

"I'm glad you did."

"Me, too," the woman admitted, looking every one of her eighty years and then a few. "I definitely feel better now than I did earlier. I think the oxygen is helping."

"Were you having a hard time breathing, Edith?"

"Not really. I just felt like air was having trouble getting into my body."

More symptoms Edith had failed to mention.

"Any weight gain?"

"She was two pounds heavier than at her last office visit a couple of weeks ago," McKenzie answered, knowing where his mind was going. "Her feet and ankles have one plus nonpitting edema and she says her wedding band," which Edith had never stopped wearing after her husband's death, "isn't tighter than normal."

While Lance checked her over from head to toe, McKenzie logged in to the computer system and began charting her notes.

"Chest is noisy." Lance had obviously heard the extra sounds in Edith's lungs, too. They were difficult to miss. "Let's get a CT of her chest and maybe a D-dimer, too."

She'd already planned to order both.

"I've added the chest CT and a BNP to her labs, and recommended proceeding with the D-dimer if her BNP is elevated." McKenzie agreed with his suggestions. "Anything else you can think of?"

He shook his head. "Maybe a sputum culture, just in case, but otherwise I think you've covered everything."

Not everything. With the human body there were so many little intricate things that could go wrong that it was impossible to cover every contingency. Especially in someone Edith's age when things were already not working as efficiently.

They stayed in Edith's room for a few more minutes, talking to her and trying to ascertain more clues about what was going on with her, then spoke with Edith's nurse to check on the reason for doing the portable chest X-ray rather than having it done in the radiology department. Apparently, the machine had been having issues. Edith's nurse was going to check with the radiologist and text McKenzie as soon as results were available.

"Anyone else you need to see before we go?" she asked Lance.

He shook his head. "I went by to check on the mayor prior to going to Edith's room."

"Oh," McKenzie acknowledged, glancing his way as they crossed the hospital parking lot. The wind nipped at her and she wished she'd changed from her lab coat into her jacket. "How is he doing?"

"He's recovering from his surgery nicely. The surgeon plans to release him to go home tomorrow as long as there are no negative changes between now and then."

"That's good."

"You saved his life."

"If I hadn't been there, you would have done so. It's really no big deal."

"He thinks it is a big deal. So does his wife. They are very grateful you were there."

McKenzie wasn't sure what Lance expected her to say. She'd just been at the right place at the right time and had helped do what had needed to be done.

"He wants us to ride on his float in the Christmas parade."

"What?"

"He invited us to ride on his float this Saturday."

"I don't want to be in the Christmas parade." Once upon a time she'd have loved to ride on a Christmas parade float.

"You a Scrooge?"

"No, but I don't want to ride on a Christmas float and wave at people who are staring at me."

Ever since her fighting parents had caused a scene at school and her entire class had stared at McKenzie, as if she had somehow been responsible, McKenzie had hated being the center of attention.

"That's fine," he said, not fazed by her reticence. "I'll do the waving and you stare at me."

"How is that supposed to keep them from staring at me?"

"I'm pretty sure everyone will be staring at the mayor and not us."

"I hope you told him no."

The corner of his mouth lifted in a half grin. "You'd hope wrong."

She stopped walking. "I'm not into being a spectacle."

She'd felt that way enough as a child thanks to her parents' antics. She wouldn't purposely put herself in that position again.

"How is participating in a community Christmas parade being a spectacle?"

She supposed he made a good point, but still…

"Besides, don't people stare at you when you run your races?"

"Long-distance running doesn't exactly draw a fan base." She started toward his car again.

"That a hint for me to come cheer you on at your next run?"

She shook her head. "I don't need anyone to cheer me on."

"What if I want to cheer you on?"

She shook her head again. She didn't want him or anyone else watching her run. She didn't want to expect someone to be there and then them possibly not show up. To run because she loved running was one thing. To run and think someone was there, supporting her, and them not really be, well, she'd felt that disappointment multiple times throughout her childhood and she'd really prefer not to go down that road again.

Some things just weren't worth repeating.

"I tell you what, if you want to come to one of my races, that's fine. But not as a cheerleader. If you want to come," she challenged, stopping at his car's passenger side, "you run."

He opened the car door and grinned. "You're inviting me to be on your team? I like the sound of that."

"There are no teams in the races I run."

"No? Well, maybe you're running in the wrong races."

"I'm not." She climbed into the seat and pulled the door to. She could hear his laughter as he rounded the car.

"You have yourself a deal, McKenzie," he said as he climbed into the driver's seat and buckled his seat belt. "I'll run with you. When's your next race?"

"I just did a half marathon on Saturday morning." She thought over her schedule a moment. "I'm signed up for one on New Year's Day morning. You should be able to still get signed up. It's a local charity run so the guidelines aren't strict."

"Length?"

"It's not a real long one, just a five-kilometer. Think you can do that?" she challenged. He was fit, but being fit didn't mean one could run. She'd learned that with a few friends who'd wanted to go with her. They'd been exercise queens, but not so much into running. McKenzie was the opposite. She was way too uncoordinated to do dancing, or anything that required group coordination, but she was a boss when it came to running.

His lips twitched with obvious amusement at her challenge. "You don't have the exclusive on running, you know."

"I've never seen you out running," she pointed out.

"You've never seen me take a shower either, but I promise you I do so on a regular basis."

Lance. In the shower. Naked. Water sluicing over his body. She gulped. Not an image she wanted in her head. "Probably all cold ones."

Maybe she needed a cold one to douse the images of him in the shower because her imagination was going hot, hot, hot.

He chuckled. "Only lately."

That got her attention. "You're taking cold showers because of me?"

"What do you think?"

"That we shouldn't be having this conversation." She stared at him, unable to help asking again. "I'm really why you need to take cold showers lately?"

He grinned. "I was only teasing, McKenzie. I haven't taken a cold shower in years."

"That I believe."

"But not that I might be rejected and need cold water?"

"I doubt you're rejected often."

"Rarely, but it does happen from time to time."

"Is that why you're here with me?"

"Because you rejected me?" He shook his head. "I'm here with you because you were smart enough to say yes to getting frozen yogurt with me."

"And real food," she reminded him as he put his car into reverse. "Don't forget you have to feed me real food before plying me with dessert."

McKenzie closed her mouth around her spoonful of frozen birthday-cake yogurt and slowly pulled the utensil from her mouth, leaving behind some of the cold, creamy substance.

"Good?"

Her gaze cut to the man sitting across the small round table from her. "What do you think?"

"That watching you eat frozen yogurt should come with a black-label warning."

"Am I dangerous to your health?"

"Just my peace of mind."

McKenzie's lips twitched. "That makes us even."

They'd gone to a local steak house and McKenzie had gotten grilled chicken, broccoli and a side salad. She'd been so full when they'd left the restaurant that if not for Lance's insistence that they do their part to support the Toys for

Tots, she'd have begged off dessert. She'd been happy to discover the old adage about there always being room for ice cream had held true for frozen yogurt. She was enjoying the cold goodness.

She was also enjoying the company.

Lance had kept their conversation light, fun. They'd talked about everything from their favorite sports teams, to which McKenzie had had to admit she didn't actually have favorites, to talking about medical school. They'd argued in fun about a new reality singing television program she'd been surprised to learn he watched. Often she'd sit and have the show on while she was logged in to the clinic's remote computer system and working on her charts. He did the same.

"I'm glad you said yes, McKenzie."

"To frozen yogurt?"

"To me."

Taking another bite, she shook her head. "I didn't say yes to you."

His eyes twinkled. "That isn't what I meant. We can take our time in that regard."

"Really?"

For once he looked completely serious. "As much time as you want and need."

"What if I never want or need 'that'?"

"Then I will be reintroduced to cold showers," he teased, taking a bite of his yogurt and not seeming at all concerned that she might not want or need "that," which contrarily irked her a bit.

"I'm not going to jump into bed with you tonight."

"I don't expect you to." He was still smiling as if they were talking about the weather rather than his sex life, or potential lack thereof.

"But if I said yes, you would jump into my bed?"

"With pleasure."

Shaking her head, she let out a long breath. "This morning, had someone told me I'd go out to dinner with you, go for dessert with you, I'd have told them they were wrong. It's going to take time to get used to the idea that we are an item."

"Does it usually take a while to get used to the idea of dating someone?"

"Not ever," she admitted.

"Why me?"

She shrugged. "I don't know. Maybe because for so long I've told myself I'm not allowed to date you."

"Because of work?"

"Amongst other things."

"Explain."

"I'm not sure I can," she admitted. How could she explain what she didn't fully understand herself? Even if she could explain it to him, she wasn't sure she'd want to. "Enough serious conversation. Tell me how you got started in community theater."

CHAPTER SEVEN

LANCE WALKED MCKENZIE to her front door, and stood on her porch yet again. This time he didn't debate with himself about whether or not he was going to kiss her.

He was going to.

What he wasn't going to do was go inside her place.

Not that he didn't want to.

He did.

Not that he didn't think there was a big part of her that wanted him to.

He did.

But she was so torn about them being together that he'd like her to be 100 percent on board when they made that step.

Why she was so torn, he wasn't sure. Neither of them were virgins. Neither of them had long-term expectations of the relationship. Just that his every gut instinct told him to take his time if that's what it took.

Took for what?

That's what he couldn't figure out.

He just knew McKenzie was different, that for the first time in a long time he really liked a woman.

Maybe for the first time since Shelby.

Guilt slammed him, just as it always did when he thought of her. What right did he have to like another woman? He didn't deserve that right. Not really. He took a deep breath and willed his mind not to go there. Not right now, although maybe he deserved to be reminded of it right now and every other living, breathing moment. Instead, he stared down into the pretty green eyes of the woman looking up at him with a thousand silent questions.

"Well?" she asked. "Are we back to my having to ask for your next move? Seriously, I gave you more credit than this."

He swallowed the lump forming in his throat. "If that were the case, what move would you ask me to make?"

McKenzie let out an exaggerated sigh. "Just kiss me and get it over with."

He tweaked his finger across her pert, upturned nose. "For that, I should just go home."

She crossed her arms. "Fine. Go home."

"See if you care?"

Her brows made a V. "What?"

"I was finishing your rant for you."

"Whatever." She rolled her eyes. "Go home, Lance. Have your shower. Cold. Hot. Lukewarm. Whatever."

Despite his earlier thoughts, he couldn't hold in his laughter at her indignation. "I intend to, but not before I kiss you good-night."

"Okay."

Okay? He smiled at her response, at the fact that she closed her eyes and waited for his mouth to cover hers, though her arms were still defensively crossed.

She was amazingly beautiful with her hat pulled down over her ears and her scarf around her neck. The temperature was only in the upper fifties, so it wasn't that cold. Just cold enough to need an outside layer.

And to cause a shiver to run down Lance's spine.

It had probably been the cold and not the anticipation of kissing McKenzie that had caused his body to quiver.

Maybe.

"Well?" She peeped at him through one eye. "Sun's going to be coming up if you don't get a move on. Time's a-wasting."

She closed her eye again and waited.

Smiling, he leaned down, saw her chin tilt toward him in anticipation, but rather than cover her lips he pressed a kiss to her forehead.

Her eyes popped open and met his, but she didn't say anything.

Her lips parted in invitation, but he still didn't take them. He kissed the corner of each eye, her cheekbones, the exposed section of her neck just above her scarf. He kissed the corners of her mouth.

She moaned, placed her gloved hands on his cheeks and stared up at him. She didn't speak, though, just stood on tiptoe while pulling him toward her, taking what she wanted.

Him.

She covered his mouth with hers and the porch shifted beneath Lance's feet. They threatened to kick up and take off on a happy flight.

Unlike their previous kisses, where he'd initiated the contact, this time it was her mouth taking the lead. Her lips demanding more. Her hands pulling him closer and closer. Her body pressing up against his.

Her wanting more, expressing that want through her body and actions.

Lance moaned. Or growled. Or made some type of strange noise deep in his throat.

Whatever the sound was, McKenzie pulled back and giggled. "What was that?"

"A mating call?"

"That was supposed to make me want to rip off your clothes and mate?"

His lips twitched. "You're telling me it didn't?"

Smiling, she shook her head. "Better go home and practice that one, big boy."

"Guess I'd better." He rubbed his thumb across her cheek. "Thank you for tonight, McKenzie."

"You paid for dinner and dessert. Everything was delicious. I'm the one who should be thanking you, again."

"You were delicious."

She laughed. "Must have been leftover frozen yogurt."

He shook his head. "I don't think so."

She met his gaze and her smile faded a little. "Tell me this isn't a bad idea."

"'This'?"

She gnawed on her lower lip. "I don't do long-term relationships, Lance. You know that. We've talked about that. This isn't going to end with lots of feel-good moments."

"I do know that and am fine with it. I'm not looking for marriage either, McKenzie. Far from it."

"Then we both understand that this isn't going anywhere between us. Not anywhere permanent or long lasting."

"We're clear." Lance wasn't such a fool that he didn't recognize that he'd only kissed her and yet he wanted McKenzie more than he recalled wanting any woman, ever.

Even Shelby.

Then again, he'd been a kid when he and Shelby had been together, barely a man. Old enough to enter into adulthood with her only to lose her before either of them had experienced the real world. Typically, when he dated, Shelby didn't play on his mind so much. Typically, when he dated, he didn't feel as involved as he already felt with McKenzie.

"I'll see you in the morning?" she asked, staring up at him curiously.

"Without a doubt."

Her smile returned. "I'm glad."

With that, she planted one last, quick kiss on his mouth then went into her house, leaving him on her front porch staring at her closed front door and wondering what the hell he was getting himself into and if he should run while he still could.

McKenzie ran as fast as she could, but her feet weren't co-operating. Each time she tried to lift her running shoe–clad foot, it was as if it weighed a ton and she didn't have the strength to do more than lean in the direction she wanted to go. She stared off into the distance. Nothing. There was nothing there. Just gray-black nothingness.

Yet, desperately, she attempted to move her feet in that direction.

Fear pumped her blood through her body.

She had to run.

Had to.

Yet, try as she might, nothing was happening.

Run, McKenzie, run before...

Before what?

She wasn't sure. There was nothing to run to. Was she running from something?

She turned, was shocked to see Lance standing behind her.

Again, she tried to move her feet, but nothing happened. Desperation pumped through her. She had to get away from him. Fast.

She glanced down at her running shoes and frowned. Gone were her running shoes and in their place were con-crete blocks where her shoes and feet should be.

What was going on?

She glanced over her shoulder and saw that Lance was casually strolling toward her. He was taking his time, not in any rush, not even breaking a sweat, but he was steadily closing the gap between them.

Grinning in that carefree way he had, he blew her a kiss and panic filled her.

People were all around, watching them, gawking, pointing and staring.

Run, McKenzie, run.

It's what she did.

What she always did.

But she'd never had concrete blocks for feet before.

Which really didn't make sense. How could her feet be concrete blocks?

Somewhere in the depths of her fuzzy mind she realized she was dreaming.

Unable to run?

People everywhere staring at her?

That wasn't a dream.

That was a nightmare.

Even if it was Lance who was closing in on her and he seemed quite happy with his pursuit and inevitable capture of her.

"The radiologist just called me with the report on Edith's CT and D-dimer." McKenzie stood in Lance's office doorway, taking him in at his desk. His brown hair was ruffled and when his gaze met hers, his eyes were as bright as the bluest sky.

"She has a pulmonary embolism?" Lance asked.

"He called you, too?"

"No, I just figured that was the case after listening to her last night and the things you said."

"That doesn't explain the blood she spat up. She shouldn't have spat up blood with a clot in her lungs. That doesn't make sense."

"You're right. Makes me wonder what else is going on. Did they get the sputum culture sent off?"

"Yes, with her first morning cough-up. Her pulmonologist is supposed to see her this morning. Her cardiologist, too."

"That's good."

Suddenly, McKenzie felt uncomfortable standing in Lance's doorway. What had she been thinking when she'd sought him out to tell him of Edith's test results?

Obviously, she hadn't been thinking.

She could have texted him Edith's results.

She'd just given in to the immediate desire to tell him, to see him, to share her anxiety over the woman's diagnosis. She really liked Edith and had witnessed Lance's affection for her, too.

"Um, well, I thought you'd want to know. I'll let you get back to work," she said, taking a step backward and feeling more and more awkward by the moment.

"Thank you, McKenzie."

Awkward.

"You're welcome." She turned, determined to get out of Dodge as quickly as possible.

"McKenzie?"

Heart pounding in her throat, she slowly turned back toward him. "Yes?"

His gaze met hers and he asked, "Dinner tonight if I don't see you before then?"

Relief washed over her.

"If you do see me before, what then? Do I not get dinner? Just dessert or something?"

He grinned. "You do keep me on my toes."

Since he was sitting down, she didn't comment, just waited on him to elaborate.

"Regardless of when we next see each other, I'd like to take you to dinner tonight, McKenzie. As you well know, I'm also good for dessert."

"Sounds like a plan," she answered, wondering why she felt so relieved that he'd asked, that they had plans to see each other after work hours. He'd been asking her for weeks and she'd been saying no. Now that she was willing to say yes, had she thought he wasn't going to ask?

"Great." His smile was bigger now, his dimples deeper. "We can discuss what we're going to wear for the Christmas parade. I'm thinking you should be a sexy elf."

"A sexy elf, hmm?" she mused, trying to visualize what he was picturing in his mind. He'd make a much sexier Santa's helper than she would. Maybe he should do the sexy-elf thing. "I haven't agreed to be in the Christmas parade," she reminded him.

"It'll be fun. The mayor's float is based on a children's story about a grumpy fellow who hates Christmas until a little girl shows him the true meaning of the holidays. It's a perfect float theme."

"I get to do weird things to my hair and wear ear and nose extensions that make me look elfish for real?" she asked with false brightness.

"You do. Don't forget the bright clothes."

She narrowed her gaze suspiciously. "And you're going to do the same?"

"I'm not sure about doing weird things to my hair." He ran his fingers through his short brown locks. "But I can get into the colorful Christmas spirit if that makes you happy."

This should be good. Seeing him in his float clothes would be worth having to come up with a costume of her own. After all, she had a secret weapon: Cecilia, who rocked makeup and costumes.

"Well, then. Sign me up for some Christmas float happiness."

Cecilia really was like a Christmas float costume secret weapon. A fairy godmother.

She walked around McKenzie, her lips twisted and her brow furrowed in deep thought.

"We can use heavy-duty bendable hair wires to wrap

your hair around to make some fancy loops." Cecelia studied McKenzie's hair. "That and lots of hair spray should do the trick."

"What about for an outfit?"

"*K-I-S-S.*"

"What?"

"Keep It Simple, Stupid. Not that you're stupid," Cecilia quickly added. "Just don't worry about trying to overdo anything. You've got less than a week to put something together. The mayor may not be expecting you to be dressed up."

"Lance says we are expected to dress up."

Cecilia's eyes lit with excitement, as if she'd been patiently waiting for the perfect opportunity to ask but had gotten distracted at the prospect of having her way with McKenzie's hair and costume makeup. "How is the good doctor?"

"Good. Very good."

Cecilia's eyes widened. "Really?"

McKenzie looked heavenward, which in this case was the glittery ceiling of Bev's Beauty Boutique. "I've kissed the man. That's it. But, yes, he was very good at that."

Cecilia let out a disappointed sight. "Just kissing?"

Her lips against Lance's could never be called "just kissing," but she wasn't going to point that out to Cecilia.

"What did you think I meant when I said he was very good?"

"You know exactly what I thought, what I was hoping for. What's holding you back?"

McKenzie shrugged. "We've barely been on three dates, and that's if you count the community Christmas show, which truly shouldn't even count but since he kissed me for the first time that night, I will." Why was she sounding so breathy and letting her sentences run together? "You think I should have already invited him between my sheets?"

"If I had someone that sexy looking at me the way that man looks at you, I'd have invited him between my sheets long ago."

McKenzie shrugged again. "There's no rush."

"No rush?" Shaking her head, Cecilia frowned. "I'm concerned."

"About me? Why?"

"For some reason you are totally throwing up walls between you and this guy. For the life of me I can't figure out why."

McKenzie glanced around the salon. There was a total of five workstations. On the other side of the salon, Bev was rolling a petite blue-haired lady's hair into tight little clips, but the other two stylists had gone to lunch, as had the manicurist. No one was paying the slightest attention to Cecilia and McKenzie's conversation. Thank goodness.

"How many times do I have to say it? I work with him. A relationship between us is complicated."

Cecilia wasn't buying it. "Only as complicated as the two of you make it."

McKenzie sank into her friend's salon chair and spun around to stare at the reflection of herself in the mirror. "I am creating problems where there aren't any, aren't I?"

"Looks that way to me. My question is why. I know you don't fall into bed with every guy you date and certainly not after just a couple of dates, but you've never had chemistry with anyone the way you do with Lance. I could practically feel the electricity zapping between you that night at the Christmas show," she pointed out. "You've never been one to create unnecessary drama. So, as your best friend, that leaves me asking myself, and you, why are you doing it now?"

True. She hadn't. Then again, she never dated anyone very long. Not that three dates classified as dating Lance for a long time. She'd certainly never dated anyone like

Lance. Not even close. He was…different. Not just that he worked with her, but something more that was hard to define and a little nerve-racking to contemplate.

"You really like him, don't you?"

At her best friend's question, McKenzie's gaze met Cecilia's in the mirror. "What's not to like?"

Cecilia grinned. "What? No argument? Uh-oh. This one has you hooked. You may decide you want to keep him around."

"That's what I'm afraid of." Then what? Eventually, he'd be ready to move on and if she were more vested in an actual relationship, she'd be hurt. Being with someone so charismatic and tempting was probably foolish to begin with.

She toyed with a strand of hair still loose from its rubber band. "So, on Saturday morning you're going to make me look like Christmas morning and then transform me into a beautiful goddess for the hospital Christmas party that evening?"

"Sure. Just call me Fairy Godmother." Cecilia's eyes widened again. "Does that mean you're going to go to the hospital Christmas party with Lance?"

McKenzie nodded. She'd just decided that for definite, despite his having mentioned it to her several times. Even if she did insist on them going separately, what would be the point other than that stubbornness he'd mentioned?

Lance stared at the cute brunette sitting on a secured chair on the back of a transfer truck flatbed that had been converted into a magical winter wonderland straight out of a children's storybook.

As was McKenzie with her intricate twisted-up hair with its battery-powered blinking multicolored minilights that were quite attention gathering for someone who'd once said she didn't want anyone staring at her, her elaborate makeup done to include a perky little nose and ear tips, and a red velvet dress fringed with white fur, white stockings and knee-high black boots that had sparkly bows added to them.

She fit in with the others on the float as if she'd been a planned part rather than a last-minute addition by the mayor. Lance liked her costume best, but admitted he was biased. The mayor and his wife stood on a built-up area of the float. They waved at the townspeople as the float made its way along the parade route.

"Tell me this isn't the highlight of your year."

"Okay. This isn't the highlight of my year," she said, but she was smiling and waving and tossing candy to the kids they passed. "Thank you for bringing candy. How did you know?"

"My favorite part of a Christmas parade was scrambling to get candy."

"Oh."

Something in her voice made him curious to know more, to understand the sadness he heard in that softly spoken word.

"Didn't your parents let you pick up candy thrown by strangers?" He kept his voice light, teasing. "On second thought, I should talk to my parents about letting me do that."

"Well, when there are big signs announcing who is on each float, it's not really like taking candy from strangers," she conceded. "But to answer your question, no, my parents didn't. This is my first ever Christmas parade."

"What?"

She'd grown up in Coopersville. The Christmas parade was an annual event and one of the highlights of the community as far as he was concerned. How could she possibly have never gone to one before?

"You heard me, elf boy."

He smiled at her teasing.

"How is it that you haven't ever gone to a Christmas parade before when I know you grew up here and the parade has been around for more decades than you have?"

She shrugged a fur-covered shoulder. "I just haven't. It's not a big deal."

But it was. He heard it in her voice.

"Did your parents not celebrate the holidays?" Not everyone did. With his own mother loving Christmas as much as he did, he could barely imagine someone not celebrating it, but he knew those odd souls were out there.

"They did," McKenzie assured him. "Just in their own unique ways."

Unique ways? His curiosity was piqued, but McKenzie's joy was rapidly fading so he didn't dig.

"Which didn't include parades or candy gathering?"

"Exactly."

"Fair enough."

"You know, I've seen half a dozen people we work with in the crowds," she pointed out. "There's Jenny Westman who works in Accounting, over there with her kids."

She smiled, waved, and tossed a handful of candy in the kids' general direction.

"I see her." He tossed a handful of individually wrapped bubble gums to the kids, too, smiling as they scrambled around to grab up the goodies. "Jenny has cute kids."

"How can you tell with the way she has them all bundled up?" McKenzie teased, still smiling. "I'm not sure I would have recognized them if she wasn't standing next to them."

"You have a point. I think she just recognized us. She's waving with one hand and pointing us out to her husband with the other."

Still holding her smiling, waving pose, McKenzie nodded.

"I imagine everyone is going to be talking about us being together on this float."

"We've had dinner together every night this week. Everyone is already talking about us."

"You're probably right."

"And the ones who aren't will be after tonight's office Christmas party."

"Why? What's happening tonight?"

"You're going as my date. Remember?"

"I remember. I just thought you meant something more."

"More than you going as my date? McKenzie, a date with me is something more."

"Ha-ha, keep telling yourself that," she warned, but she was smiling and not just in her waving-at-the-crowds way of smiling. Her gaze cut to him and her smile dazzled more than any jewel.

"You look great, by the way," he said.

"Thanks. I owe it all to Cecilia. She worked hard putting this together and got to my house at seven this morning to do my hair and makeup. She came up with the lights and promised me that my hair, the real and the fake she brought with her to make it look so poufy and elaborate, wouldn't catch fire. I admit I was a bit worried when she told me she was stringing lights through my hair."

"Like I said, you look amazing and are sure to help the mayor win best float. Cecilia's good."

"Yep. Works at Bev's Beauty Boutique. Just in case you ever need a cut and style or string of Christmas lights dangled above your head on twisted-up fake hair."

"I'll keep that in mind." He reached over and took her gloved hand in his and gave it a squeeze. "I'm glad you agreed to do this."

She didn't look at him, but admitted, "Me, too."

When they reached the final point of the parade, the driver parked the eighteen-wheel truck that had pulled the float. Lance jumped down and held his hand out to assist McKenzie. The mayor and his wife soon joined them. He'd just been discharged from the hospital the day before and probably shouldn't have been out in the parade, but the man had insisted on participating.

"Thank you both for being my honored guests," he praised them in a hoarse, weakened voice. He shook Lance's hand.

"It was our pleasure," Lance assured the man he'd checked on several times throughout his hospital stay despite the fact that he wasn't a patient of their clinic. He genuinely liked the mayor and had voted for him in the last election.

The mayor turned to McKenzie. "Thank you for saving my life, young lady. There'd have been no Christmas cheer this year in my household if not for you."

McKenzie's cheeks brightened to nearly the same color as her plush red dress. "You're welcome, but Dr. Spencer did just as much to save your life as I did. He's the one who did the Heimlich maneuver and your chest compressions."

"You were the one who revived me. Dr. Spencer has told me on more than one occasion that your actions are directly responsible for my still being here."

McKenzie glanced at him in question and Lance winked.

"If there's ever anything we can do." This came from the mayor's wife. "Just let us know. We are forever indebted to you both. You're our Christmas angels."

"We're good, but thank you," Lance and McKenzie both assured them.

"Amazing costume," the mayor's wife praised McKenzie further.

They talked for a few more minutes to those who'd been on the mayor's float, then walked toward the square where the rest of the parade was still passing.

"If it's okay, I'd like to swing by to see Cecelia at the shop."

"No problem," he assured her. "I need to thank her for making you look so irresistibly cute."

McKenzie grimaced. "Cute is not how a woman wants to be described."

"Well, you already had beautiful, sexy, desirable, intelligent, brilliant, gorgeous, breathtaking—"

"You can stop anytime," she interrupted, laughing.

"Amazing, lickable—"

"Did you just say *lickable*?" she interrupted again.

He paused, frowned at her. "Lickable? Surely not."

"Surely so."

"I said *likable*. Not lickable."

"You said lickable."

He did his best to keep a straight face. "You'd think with those elongated ears you'd have better hearing."

She touched one of her pointy ears. "You'd think."

"So maybe I'll just thank her for your costume that's lit up my day so far."

McKenzie reached up and touched her hair. "That would be accurate, at least."

"All the other was, too." Before she could argue, he grabbed her hand and held it as they resumed walking toward Bev's Beauty Boutique.

The wind was a little chilly, but overall the weather was a fairly mild December day in mid-Georgia.

"Oh, goodness, look at you two," Bev gushed in her gravelly voice when McKenzie and Lance walked up to the shop. Lance had met her at a charity function a time or two over the years he'd been in Coopersville. A likable woman even if he did always have to take a step back because of her smoky breath.

Bev and a couple other women were outside the shop, watching the remainder of the parade pass.

"Cecilia, you outdid yourself, girl! McKenzie, you look amazing." Bev, a woman who'd smoked her way to looking older than she was, ran her gaze over Lance's trousers, jacket, and big Christmas bow tie. He'd borrowed some fake ears and a nose tip from the community center costume room from a play they'd put on several years before. "I'm pretty sure you're hotter than Georgia asphalt in mid-July."

McKenzie laughed out loud at the woman's assessment of him. Lance just smiled and thanked her for her hoarse compliment.

"You do look amazing," Cecelia praised her friend. "Even if I do say so myself." She pulled out her cell phone. "I want a picture."

"You took photos this morning," McKenzie reminded as her friend held her cell phone out in front of her.

"Yeah, but that was just you," Cecilia pointed out. "I want pictures of you two together, too. Y'all are the cutest Christmas couple ever."

Reluctantly, McKenzie posed for her friend, then seemed to loosen up a little when she pulled Lance over to where she stood. "Come on, elf boy. You heard her. She wants pictures of us both. If I have to do this, so do you."

Lance wasn't reluctant at all. He wrapped his arm around McKenzie and smiled for the camera while Cecilia took their first photos together.

Their first. Did that mean he thought there would be other occasions for them to be photographed together? Did that imply that he wanted those memories with her captured forever?

"Do something other than smile," Cecilia ordered, looking at them from above her held-out phone.

Lance turned to McKenzie to follow her lead. Her gaze met his, and she shrugged, then broke off a sprig of mistletoe from the salon's door decoration. She held up the greenery, then pulled him to her, did a classic one-leg-kicked-up pose, and planted a kiss right on his cheek with her eyes toward her friend.

No doubt Cecilia's phone camera flash caught his surprise.

He quickly recovered and got into the spirit of things by pointing at the mistletoe McKenzie held and giving an *Oh, yeah* thumbs-up, then posed for several goofy shots and laughed harder than he probably should have at their antics.

All the women and a few spectators laughed and applauded them. A few kids wanted to pose for photos with them, especially McKenzie.

"Is your hair real?" a little girl asked, staring at the twisted-up loops of hair and string of minilights.

"Part of it is real, but I don't normally wear it this way. Just on special days."

"Like on Christmas parade days?" the child asked.

"Exactly."

When they'd finished visiting with her friends, McKenzie hugged Cecilia and thanked her again.

"Don't forget to forward me those pictures," she requested with one last hug.

"I may be calling on you to help with some of our charity events. We're always needing help with costumes and you're good," Lance praised.

Cecilia beamed. "Thank you."

The parade ended and the crowd began to disperse. Customers came to the shop to have their ritual Saturday morning hair appointments and the stylists went back into the salon.

"Now what?" McKenzie asked, turning to face him. Her cheeks glowed with happiness and she looked as if she was having the time of her life.

"Anything you want."

She laughed. "If only I could think of something evil and diabolical."

He took her gloved hand into his. "I'm not worried."

"You should be."

She tried to look evil and diabolical, but only managed to look cute. He lifted her hand to his mouth and pressed a kiss to her fuzzy glove.

"You wouldn't hurt a fly."

"I definitely would," she contradicted. "I don't like flies."

"Okay, Miss Evil and Diabolical Fly-Killer, let's go grab some hot chocolate and see what the Christmas booths have for sale that we can snag."

"Sounds wonderful."

CHAPTER EIGHT

"YOU LOOKED AMAZING TODAY," Cecilia told her as she ran a makeup pencil over McKenzie's brow with the precision of an artist working on a masterpiece.

"Thanks to you and the fabulous work you did getting me ready for the mayor's float," McKenzie agreed, trying to hold perfectly still so she didn't mess up what her friend was doing to her face.

"I have to admit, I had fun. Then again, I had a lot to work with."

"Yeah, right," McKenzie snorted. "Let's just hope you can pull off another miracle for tonight, too."

"For your work Christmas party?"

"Yes." She cut her eyes to her friend. "What did you think I meant?"

"You've never asked me to help doll you up in the past for a mere work party."

"This one is different."

"Because of Lance?"

Because of Lance. Yes, it seemed that most everything this week had been because of Lance. Lots of smiles. Lots of hot kisses. Lots of anticipation and wondering if tonight was the night they'd do more than "mouth-to-mouth."

"I suppose so. Can't a girl just want to look her best?"

"Depends on what she's wanting to look her best for."

"For my party."

"And afterward?"

"Well, I'm hoping not to turn into a pumpkin at midnight, if that's what you're asking."

"No pumpkins," Cecilia promised. "Wrong holiday. But what about that mistletoe this morning?"

"What about it?"

"You've gone to dinner every night this week, ridden on a Christmas float with him, and you are going as his date to the Christmas party. That's big, McKenzie. For you, that's huge. What changed?"

"Nothing."

"Something has to have changed. You were saying no to the guy left and right only a week ago."

"You were the one who said I was crazy for not going out with him."

"You *were* crazy for not going out with him. He seems like a great guy. Lots of fun, hot, and crazy about my bestie. I like him."

"You've only been around him twice," McKenzie reminded.

"During which times he helped save a man's life and made you laugh and smile more than I've seen you do in years."

There was that.

"I was in character."

"Yeah right." Cecilia threw McKenzie's words back at her. "If I'd been you, I'd have used that mistletoe for more than a kiss on the cheek."

"I'm sure you would have."

"But you didn't need to, did you?"

"I'm not the kind of girl to kiss and tell." Which was hilarious because Cecilia had been her best friend since before her first kiss and she'd told her about pretty much all her major life events. Plus, she had already told Cecilia that she and Lance had kissed.

Cecilia leaned back, studied McKenzie's face, then went back to stroking a brush across her cheeks. "Even if you hadn't already told me that you kissed Lance on the night of the Christmas show, I'd know you had."

"How would you know that?"

"I can tell. The same as I can tell that, despite our conversation the other day, what you still haven't done is have sex with him."

Could Cecilia see inside her head or did her friend just know her that well?

"And how is it you know that?"

Cecilia's penciled on brow arches. "Am I wrong?"

"No," she admitted. "I've not had sex with him."

Not that he'd made any real plays to get into her bed. He hadn't. Which surprised her.

"The tension between you two is unreal."

"Tension? We weren't fighting today."

"Sexual tension, McKenzie. It's so thick between you two that you could cut it with a knife."

There was that. Which made his lack of pushing beyond their nightly kisses even more difficult to understand.

"I see you're not denying it."

"Would there be any point?"

"None." Cecilia leaned back again and smiled at what she saw. She held a hand mirror up for McKenzie to see what she'd done. "Perfect."

McKenzie stared at her reflection. Cecilia had done wonders with her face. McKenzie rarely wore more than just mascara and a shiny lip gloss that she liked the scent of. Cecilia had plucked, brushed, drawn and done her face up to the point where McKenzie barely recognized the glamorous woman staring back at her. "Wow."

"How much do you want to bet that when Lance sees

you he'll want to forget the party and just stay here and party with you?"

"Not gonna happen." Not on her part and, based on the past week, not on his part either. But anticipation filled her at the thought of Lance seeing her at her best. "Help me into my dress?"

"Definitely. I want to see what underwear you're wearing."

McKenzie's face caught on fire. Busted. "What?"

"You heard me," Cecilia brooked no argument. "I'll know your intentions by your underwear."

McKenzie sighed and slipped off her robe.

Grinning, Cecilia rubbed her hands together. "Now that's what I'm talking about."

"This doesn't mean a thing, you know."

"Of course it doesn't. That's why you aren't wearing granny panties."

McKenzie stuck her tongue out at her friend. "I never wear granny panties."

"Yeah, well, you don't usually wear sexy thongs either, but you are tonight."

"Works better with the material of my dress. No unsightly panty lines that way."

Cecilia had the audacity to laugh. "Keep telling yourself that."

"Fine. I will. Think what you like."

Cecilia laughed again. "Here, let's get you into your dress, let me do any necessary last-minute hair fixes, and then I'm out of here before Dr. Wonderful shows up."

"He's not that wonderful," McKenzie countered.

"Sure he's not. That's why you're a nervous wreck and wearing barely-there panties and a matching bra."

Cecilia laughed and slid McKenzie's sparkly green dress over her head and tugged it downward.

"A real best friend wouldn't point out such things," Mc-

Kenzie pointed out to the woman who'd been a constant in her life since kindergarten. "You know, it's not too late to trade you in for a less annoying model."

Cecilia's loud laughter said she was real worried.

"Have I told you how beautiful you look?"

"Only about a dozen times." McKenzie ran her gaze over Lance. He had gone all out and was wearing a black suit that fit so well she wondered if it was tailor-made. He'd washed away all traces of his Christmas parade costume. His hair had a hint of curl, his eyes a twinkle, and his lips a constant smile. "Have I mentioned how handsome you look in your suit?"

"A time or two." He grinned. "I'm the envy of every man in the building."

"Hardly."

"It's true. You look absolutely stunning."

"Cecilia gets all the credit. She's the miracle worker. I sure can't pull off this…" she gestured to her face and hair "…without her waving her magic wand."

"Your fairy godmother, huh?"

"That's what I've called her this week."

"She's definitely talented," he agreed. "Then again, she had a lot to work with because on your worst day, you're beautiful, McKenzie."

"That does it. No more spiked Christmas punch for you." She made a play for his glass, but he kept it out of her reach.

"Is the punch really spiked?"

"It must be," she assured him, "for you to be spouting so many compliments."

He waggled his brows and took another drink. "I don't think so."

The Christmas party was being held in a local hotel's conference room. There were about two hundred employees in total who worked for the clinic. With those employees and their significant others, the party was going full swing and was full of loud commotion from all directions.

Several of their coworkers had commented on how great they looked tonight, how great they'd looked in the Christmas parade, how excited they were that they were a couple.

Those comments made McKenzie want to squirm in her three-inch heels. All their coworkers now knew without a doubt that they were seeing each other as more than friends.

She'd known this would happen. She'd allowed this to happen.

Several of her female coworkers stared at her with outright envy that she was with Lance. She couldn't blame them. He was gorgeous, fun, intelligent and charming. He didn't seem to notice any of their attention, just stayed close to McKenzie's side and tended to her every need.

Well, almost every need.

Because more and more she'd been thinking of Cecilia's teasing. Yeah, her green dress fit her like a glove right down to where it flared into a floaty skirt that twirled around her thighs when she moved just right. But she hadn't had to wear teeny-tiny underwear because of the dress. She'd worn them because...

"That's the first time I've not seen a smile on your face all evening," Lance whispered close to her ear.

"Sorry," she apologized, immediately smiling. "I was just thinking."

Which, of course, led to him asking what she'd been thinking about.

She just smiled a little brighter, grabbed his hand, and tugged him toward the dance floor. "Dance with me?"

"I thought you'd never ask," he teased, leading her out onto the crowded dance floor. "I've been itching to have you in my arms all evening."

"All you had to do was ask."

"Well, part of me was concerned about the consequences of holding you close."

"Consequences?" She stared into his eyes, saw the truth there, then widened her eyes. "Oh."

"Yeah, oh."

"I guess it's a good thing girls don't have to worry about such things."

His eyes remained locked with hers, half teasing, half serious. "Would that be a problem for you, McKenzie?"

A problem?

Her chin lifted. "I'm not frigid, if that's what you're asking."

"It wasn't, but it's good to know." He pulled her close and they swayed back and forth to the beat of the music.

"You smell good," she told him, trying not to completely bury her face in his neck just to fill her senses totally with the scent of him.

"I was just thinking the same thing about you. What perfume are you wearing?"

"Cecilia sprayed me with some stuff earlier. I honestly don't know what it's called, just that she said it was guaranteed to drive you crazy. Of course, she didn't tell me that until after she'd hit me with a spray."

He nuzzled against her hair. "She was right."

"Feeling a little crazy?"

"With your body rubbed up against mine? Oh, yeah."

She laughed. "I'll let her know the stuff works."

"Pretty sure if you had nothing on at all I'd be feeling just as crazy. Actually, if you had nothing on at all, my current level of crazy would be kid's stuff in comparison."

She wiggled closer against him. "Well, that makes sense. We're both just kids at heart."

"True, that." His hands rubbed against her low back. "Were you thinking about our coworkers just a few minutes ago?"

She knew when he meant and at that time it hadn't been thoughts of their coworkers that had robbed her of her smile. No, it had been thoughts of what she was anticipating happening later in the evening. Not that she was sure that's what would happen, but she'd questioned it enough that she'd shaved, lotioned, powdered, perfumed and dressed in her sexiest underwear.

Because all week Lance had kissed her good-night, deep, thorough passionate kisses that had left her longing for more. She hadn't invited him in and he hadn't pushed. Just hot good-night kisses night after night that left her confused and aching.

Mostly, she just didn't understand why he hadn't attempted to talk his way into her bed. Or at least into her house. He'd still not made it off the front porch.

He might not push for more tonight either. She was okay with it if he didn't. It was just that something had felt different between them today on the Christmas float, and afterward when they'd weaved their way from one booth to another. All week she'd felt as if she was building up to something great. From the moment he'd picked her up at her house this evening and had been so obviously pleased with the way she looked and how she'd greeted him—with lots of smiles—the feeling had taken root inside her that tonight held magical possibilities that she wasn't sure she really wanted in the long run, but in the short term, oh, yeah, she wanted Lance something fierce, thus the itsy-bitsy, barely-there thong.

"Should I be concerned about how quiet you are?" he asked.

"Nope. I'm just enjoying the dance."

"Any regrets?"

His question caught her off guard and she pulled back enough to where she could see his face. "About?"

"Coming to the party with me."

"Not yet."

He chuckled. "You expecting that to change?"

"Depends on your behavior between now and the time we leave."

"Then I guess I better be on my best, eh?"

"Something like that."

Not that she could imagine Lance not being on his best behavior at all times. He was always smiling, doing something to help others. Never had she met a man who volunteered more. It was as if his life's mission was to do as much good as he possibly could in the world. Or at least within their small community.

The music changed to an upbeat number and they danced to a few more songs. The emcee for the evening stopped the music and made several announcements, gave away a few raffle items.

"Now, folks." The emcee garnered their attention. "I'd like to call Dr. Lance Spencer to the stage."

Lance glanced at her. "Do you know anything about this?"

McKenzie shook her head. She didn't have a clue.

Pulling McKenzie along with him, he headed up toward the makeshift stage. She managed to free her hand just before he stepped up onto the stage. No way was he taking her up there with him. Who knew what was about to happen? Maybe he had won a raffle or special door prize or something.

"Dr. Spencer," the emcee continued, "I'm told you make a mean emcee."

"I wouldn't say 'mean,'" Lance corrected, laughing.

"Well, a little birdie tells me you've been known to rock a karaoke machine and requested you sing to kick off our karaoke for the evening."

Lance glanced at McKenzie, but she shook her head. That little birdie wasn't her.

Always in the spirit of things, Lance shrugged, and told the emcee the name of a song. As the music started, microphone in hand, he stepped off the stage and took McKenzie's hand again.

"I need a singing partner."

Her heart in her nonsinging throat, McKenzie shook her head. He wasn't doing this. She didn't want to make a spectacle of them by pulling her hand free of his, but her feet were about to take off at any moment, which meant he was either coming with her, hands clasped and all, or she'd be doing exactly that.

"Come on," he encouraged. "Don't be shy. Sing with me, McKenzie. It'll be fun."

By this time, the crowd was also really into the spirit of things and urging her onto the stage. She heard a female doctor whose office was right next to hers call out for her to go for it.

McKenzie's heart sank. She wasn't going to be able to run away. Not this time. She was surrounded by her coworkers. Her hand was held by Lance.

She was going to have to go onstage and sing. With Lance. Nothing like a little contrast to keep things interesting.

A singer she was not.

She closed her eyes.

What had been a great night had just gone sour. Very, *very* sour.

She blamed Lance.

Lance realized he'd made a mistake the moment he'd put McKenzie on the spot. Unfortunately, his request wasn't something she could easily refuse with their coworkers now cheering for her to join him. She could either sing or be seen as a total party pooper—which she wasn't and he knew she'd resent being labeled as one.

McKenzie's eyes flashed with fear and he wasn't sure what all else.

He'd messed up big time.

Faking a smile, she stepped up onto the stage with him. He still held her hand. Her palm was sweaty and her fingers threatened to slip free. He gave her a reassuring squeeze. She didn't even look at him.

Lance sang and McKenzie came through from time to time, filling the backup role rather than taking a lead with him, as he'd initially hoped. Mostly, she mumbled, except during the chorus. With almost everyone in the crowd singing along, too, maybe no one noticed.

McKenzie noticed, though. The moment the song was over, she gave him the evil eye. "For the record, I don't sing and if you ever do that to me again, it'll be the last time."

"That's funny," he teased, planning to keep their conversation light, to beg her forgiveness if he needed to. "I just heard you do exactly that."

"Only a tone-deaf lunatic would call what I just did singing."

"I thought you sounded good."

"You don't count."

"Ouch." He put his hand over his heart as if she'd delivered a fatal blow. "My references say I count."

She flashed an annoyed look his way. "You're really going to have to get over those references."

"Or use them as a shield against the walloping you seem determined to deliver to me."

"Not everyone enjoys being the center of attention."

"Tell me the truth. You didn't have fun onstage just then? Not even a little?" he coaxed.

McKenzie stared at him as if he was crazy. He *was* crazy.

"I detested being onstage in front of my coworkers." She frowned as they moved onto the dance floor. Her body remained rigid, rather than relaxing against his like it had during their earlier dances. "For the record, I really don't like people staring at me. Put it down to bad childhood memories of when my parents thrust me into situations where I got a lot of unwanted attention."

When he'd gone after her to sing with him, he'd never considered that she might not enjoy being onstage. He'd just selfishly wanted her with him.

"I'm sorry, McKenzie. If I'd known how you felt, I wouldn't have put you in the spotlight that way. I definitely would never intentionally upset you. It was all in fun, to kick off the night's karaoke. That's all."

"I know you didn't intentionally pull me up there to upset me," she admitted. "I just prefer you not to put me in situations where all eyes are on me. I have enough bad childhood flashbacks as it is."

"What kind of childhood flashbacks?"

"Just situations where my parents would yell and scream at each other regardless of where we were and no matter who was around. Way too often all eyes would be on me while they had a knock-down, drag-out. When people stare at me, it gives me that same feeling of humiliation and mortification."

"I'm sorry your parents did that to you and that I made those negative feelings come to surface. But, for the record, maybe you're finally getting past those old hang-ups because you were smiling." She had been smiling. Mumbling and smiling.

"I was faking it."

"Ouch." His hand went to his chest and he pretended

to receive another mortal blow. "Not good when a man's woman has to fake it."

"Exactly. So you should be careful what situations you put me into where I might have to fake other things," she warned with a half smile. "I don't sing. I barely dance. Take note of it."

He pulled her to him, his hand low on her back, holding her close. "You dance quite nicely when you aren't in rigor mortis. However, I'll make a note. No more singing and barely dancing. Got it."

"Good."

"Also, for the record, when I put you in a certain situation, there will be no need for faking it."

Her chin tilted up and she arched a brow in challenge. "How can you be so sure?"

"Because I'll use every ounce of skill, every ounce of sheer will, every ounce of energy I have to make sure I blow your mind," he whispered close for her ears only. "My pleasure will be seeing your pleasure. Feeling your pleasure."

"That sounds…fun. Maybe you should have tried your hand at that instead of pulling me onstage with you."

He swallowed. Was she saying…?

"I want you, McKenzie. I haven't pushed because I know you still have a lot of mixed emotions about being with me, but when you're ready I want to make love to you. I've made no pretense about that."

"Sex. You want to have sex with me," she corrected, resting her forehead against his chin. "I'll let you know when I'm ready."

Lance's heart beat like a drum against his rib cage. "I'll be waiting."

"Don't hold your breath."

"I'd rather hold yours."

That had her looking up.

"Kiss me, McKenzie."

"Here? Now? On the dance floor? Around our coworkers? Are you crazy?"

He glanced around the dim room. The dance floor was crowded with couples, some of them stealing kisses. There were some single women who were dancing in a circle off to one side of the dance floor. One of the admin girls currently had the microphone and was belting out a tune. No one was paying them any attention.

McKenzie's gaze followed his, no doubt drawing the same conclusions, but she shook her head anyway. "No. I'm not one of those girls who is into public displays of affection."

"You kissed me in front of Bev's Beauty Boutique."

"That was different."

"How was that different? Other than it being in broad daylight and in the middle of the square with half the town in the near vicinity?"

"I can't explain how that was different, but it was." Her lower lip disappeared between her teeth. "Don't push me on this, please."

He sighed. "It would probably have been a bad idea for you to kiss me here, anyway."

"Why is that?"

Did she really not know how much she affected him? How much he was having to fight sweeping her up into his arms and carrying her out of the ballroom and straight to the first private place he could find where he could run his fingers beneath her sparkly green dress?

"I think I've already mentioned how much I want you and the effect you have on me."

"But... Oh." Her eyes widened as she moved against him.

"Yeah. Oh."

To his surprise, her body relaxed and he'd swear the

noise that came out of her mouth was a giggle. Not that McKenzie seemed the giggling type, but that's what the sound had most resembled.

Regardless, her arms relaxed around his neck and just to prove how ornery she was and to his total surprise her lips met his in a soft kiss that only lasted a few seconds but took his breath and made his knees weak.

"There," she taunted. "I kissed you in public."

"Not sure what made you change your mind, but thank you." He studied her expression and he'd swear there was a mischievous glint in her eyes. "I think. Because if I didn't know better I'd think you were trying to set me up for embarrassment."

There was the sound again. Definitely a giggle. "Would I do that after our conversation, with you pointing out the obvious differences in the way our bodies react?"

A grin tugged at his lips. "Yeah, you would."

Her eyes sparkled. "Did it work?"

He pulled her close and let her feel for herself that his body was indeed reacting to her, making him uncomfortable in the process. Then again, he'd left her front porch this way every night the past week.

She tilted her face toward him. "I think it did."

"You think?" He shook his head, then stroked his finger across her cheek.

He held her close until the slow dance ended then they moved to a couple of fast songs. Despite what she'd said, McKenzie could dance. She could definitely sing too if she wouldn't let her own self-doubt get in the way.

Laughing, McKenzie fell into his arms. "Hey, Lance?"

"Hmm?" he asked, kissing the top of her head just because he could, because it felt right and wonderful.

"I'm ready."

"Already?" He'd figured they'd be one of the last to

leave, not one of the first. Still, if she was done partying, he'd take her home. Then he met her gaze and what she meant glittered brightly in her emerald eyes. "Really?"

She nodded. "Let's get our coats, please."

"Yes, ma'am."

"Such good manners," she praised.

Lance grinned. "Just wait until I show you what else I'm good at."

CHAPTER NINE

YES, IT HAD been a while since she'd had sex, but McKenzie wasn't a virgin. She enjoyed sex, was athletic enough to have good stamina and a good healthy drive so she felt she was decent in the sack. So why was she suddenly so nervous?

Because she'd essentially agreed to have sex with Lance.

With Lance!

Wasn't that what the dress, the hair and makeup, *the sexy undies* had all been about? Leading up to his taking them off her, kissing her body, running his fingers though her hair, making her sweat from the intensity of their coming together?

Sex with Lance.

Lance, who did everything perfectly.

He looked perfect.

Danced perfectly.

Doctored perfectly.

Made love perfectly?

That was the question.

She gulped and had to fight to keep her eyes on the road and off the man driving his car toward her house. He hadn't looked at her and seemed to have no desire to make small talk, which she appreciated. He was as lost in his thoughts as she was.

What was he thinking?

About sex? With her?

Sometimes she wondered why he even bothered. He'd been asking her out for weeks before she'd agreed to go to the Christmas show at the community center. Why hadn't he just moved on to someone else who was more agreeable?

Ha. She was agreeable tonight. She was practically throwing herself at him.

When he'd realized what she'd meant, he'd taken her hand and, with a determined gleam in his eyes, had made a beeline for their coats, not stopping to chat with any of their coworkers and friends as they'd left.

She took a deep breath.

Lance asked, "Second thoughts?"

She glanced toward him. "No, but I feel like a teenager sneaking off from a high school dance to mess around."

He wasn't looking at her, but she'd swear Lance's face paled, that his grip on the steering wheel tightened to the point his skin stretched white over his knuckles.

When he didn't comment, she asked, "You?"

"No regrets, but we don't have to do this if you're not sure."

"I'm sure." He still looked way tenser than she felt a man on his way to getting what he'd been supposedly wanting for weeks should look. Which made her uneasy. Maybe they were talking too much and not having enough action.

Maybe she was boring him with all her conversation.

They were still another ten minutes from her house. What were they supposed to do during the drive?

Then again, she wasn't the one driving so the possibilities were only limited by her imagination.

She'd always had a good imagination. A vivid imagination.

She wiggled in the seat, enjoying the car's seat warmers. "Nice seaters you've got here."

His gaze flicked her way. "Seaters?"

"Seat heaters. Yours are awesome." Seat belt still in place, she twisted as best she could toward him and wiggled her hips. "I'm feeling all toasty warm."

He kept his eyes on the road, but his throat worked and his fingers flexed along the steering wheel. "Things getting hot down there?"

Yes, this was much better than their terse silence. This was fun. As fun as she wanted to make it.

As fun as she could imagine it.

With Lance her imagination was working overtime.

Odd because even though the thought of sex with him made her nervous, she felt no hesitation in unbuttoning her coat and slipping her arms free, and running her palms down her waist, hips, thighs, letting her fingers tease her skirt hem.

"Maybe. Give me your hand and I'll let you check for yourself."

"McKenzie." Her name came out as half plea, half groan. "I need to concentrate on the road. I don't want to wreck."

"You won't. I only need one hand. You keep your eyes on the road and your other hand on the steering wheel. No worries. I'll take good care of you."

"You think I can touch your body and not look?" His voice sounded strained.

She liked it that his voice sounded strained, that what she was doing was having a profound effect on him. "Can't you?"

"I'm not sure." He sounded as if he really wasn't.

Which made McKenzie giddy inside. He wanted her. Really wanted her. She knew this, but seeing the reality of his desire was something more, was the cherry on top.

"Let's find out." She reached for him and he let her pull his right hand to her thigh. "See, I have faith in your ability to let your fingers have some fun. You've got this."

"Fun? Is that what you call between your legs?"

Excited from how much she could see he wanted her, she reached her free hand out and ran her fingers over his fly. "It had better be what I'm calling between your legs by morning."

"McKenzie." This time her name was a tortured croak.

She smiled, liking the hard fullness she brushed her fingertips over. That was going to be hers before the sun came up. Oh, yeah. He really was perfect.

"You're testing my willpower," he ground out through gritted teeth when her fingers lingered, exploring what she'd found and become fascinated by.

That made two of them. Her willpower was in a shambles. How she'd gone from teasing to totally turned on she wasn't sure, but she had. So much so that she wiggled against the seat again, causing his hand to shift on her thigh and make goose bumps on her skin.

"I have no doubt that you've never failed a test." She placed her free hand over his and guided him beneath the hem of her dress.

"There's always a first."

"Not this time," she told him, gliding his hand between her thighs to where she blazed hotly, and not from the car's seat warmers.

"You sure about that?"

"Positive," she assured him, "because if you lose your willpower we have to stop, and where's the fun in that?"

"Fun being where my fingers are?"

"Exactly." She shifted, bringing him into full contact with those itty-bitty panties she'd put on earlier.

"If I get pulled over for speeding to get us home quicker?"

She squeezed her buttocks together in a Kegel, pressing against his fingers. "Not sure how you'd explain to the officer why you were going so fast."

"I'd tell him to look in my passenger seat and he'd understand just fine."

For all his talk, the speedometer stayed at the speed limit, which she kind of liked. Safety mattered. Even when your passenger was seducing you. That he wasn't gunning the engine of the sports car surprised her, though. She'd have bet money he'd be a speed demon behind the wheel, but she couldn't think of a time she'd been in his car when he'd been going too fast or pulling any careless stunts.

His thumb brushed lightly over her pubic bone and she moaned, forgetting all about safety.

She gripped his thigh and squeezed. "That feels good."

"I couldn't tell."

He didn't have to look at her for her to know he was smiling, pleased with her body's reaction to his touch. She heard his pleasure in his voice, felt it in the way his fingers toyed over the barely-there satin material.

"Might be time to turn that seater off since you're already steamy down there."

She tilted her hips toward his touch. "Might be, but I'm sure I could get hotter."

"You think?"

"I'm hoping."

He slowed the car and turned into her street. "Thank God we're almost there."

"Not even close," she teased. "But if you move those fingers just so, maybe."

"McKenzie." Her name was torn from deep within him. "You're killing me."

His fingers said otherwise. His fingers were little adventurers, exploring uncharted territory, staking claims in the wake of his touch.

She closed her eyes, holding on to his thigh, spreading her legs to give him better access. Gentle back-and-forth movements created cataclysmic earthquakes throughout her body.

Yearnings to rip off her clothes hit her. To rip off *his* clothes, right then, in the car, to give him free access to touch with no material in the way.

Why couldn't she?

Why couldn't she take her panties off?

That wasn't something she'd ever done before, but she was an adult, a responsible one usually. If she wanted to suddenly go commando, she could do that, right?

She hiked her dress up around her thighs, looped her fingers through the tiny straps of her thong and wiggled them down her legs. She probably looked ridiculous raised up off the seat to remove them, but who cared?

His eyes were on the road and now there was nothing to keep him from touching her. Not her panties, but her, as in skin to skin. She needed that. His skin against hers. His touch on her aching flesh.

"If I were a stronger man, I'd make you wait until we're at least in your driveway before I touched you for real," he warned.

"Good thing you're not a stronger man," she replied as his fingers slid home. "Very good thing."

His touch was light, just gentle strokes teasing her.

"This isn't fair," he complained.

"Life isn't fair. Get over it."

He laughed. "No sympathy from you."

"Hey, you've been trying to get in my pants for weeks now. Why would I feel sympathetic toward you when you're getting what you want?"

"I want more than to get into your pants, McKenzie. I want a relationship with you."

"Here's a news flash for you—if you're in my pants, you're in a relationship with me."

"For thirty days or less?" he asked.

"I'm not putting a time limit on our relationship. Move your fingers faster."

"Not until you promise you'll give me two months."

Two months? Why two months?

"This isn't as business negotiation."

"True," he agreed. "But if you want my fingers to do more than skim the surface, you'll give me your word. I want two months. Not a day less. Not a day more."

She moved against him, trying to get the friction she craved. "Two months?"

"Two months."

Ugh. He was pushing for more than she usually gave. It figured. Then again, what was two months in the grand scheme of life?

"I don't have to agree to this to get what I want. It's not as if you're going to turn down what I'm offering."

He chuckled. "Confident, aren't you?"

"Of that? Yes, you're a man."

"I won't be used for sex, McKenzie."

"Isn't that usually the woman's line?"

"These are modern times and you're a modern woman."

She arched further against his hand. "Not that modern."

"Two months?" He teased her most sensitive area with the slightest flick of his finger.

"Fine," she sighed, moving against his fingers. "You can have two months, but I won't promise a day more."

He turned into her driveway, amazing since she hadn't even realized they were that close to her house. Hadn't even recalled that they were in her street or even on the planet, for that matter. All that existed was the two of them inside his car.

He killed the engine, turned toward her, and moved her thighs apart, touching where she ached.

"I knew you could find it if you tried hard enough," she teased breathlessly.

"Oh, I'm definitely hard enough."

She reached out and touched him again. He was right. He definitely was.

Lance leaned toward her, taking her mouth as his fingers worked magic. Sparkles and rainbows and shooting-stars magic.

Her inner thighs clenched. Her eyes squeezed tight then opened wide.

Her body melted in all the right places in a powerful orgasmic wave that turned her body inside out. Or it felt like it at any rate.

Sucking in much-needed oxygen, she met his smug gaze.

Two months might not be nearly enough time if that was a preview of the main event.

Bodies tangled, Lance and McKenzie tossed a half dozen pillows off her bed and onto the floor with their free hands. A trail of clothes marked their path from the front door to her bed. His. Hers.

"I want you, McKenzie," he breathed, his hand at the base of her neck as his mouth took hers again. Long and hard, he kissed her.

McKenzie was positive she'd never been kissed so possessively, never been kissed so completely.

Even when his mouth lifted from hers, she didn't answer him verbally. She wasn't sure her vocal cords would even work if she tried.

Her hands worked, though. As did her lips. She touched Lance and kissed him, exploring the strong lines of his neck, his shoulders, his chest.

"So beautiful."

Had she said that or had he? She wasn't sure.

His hands were on her breasts, cupping her bottom, everywhere, and yet not nearly all the places she wanted to be touched.

"More," she cried, desperation filling her when it was him she wanted, him she needed. "Please. Now, Lance. I want you now."

Maybe her desperation was evident in her tone or maybe he was just as desperate because he pushed her back onto the bed, put on the condom he'd tossed onto the nightstand when they'd first entered the room, then crawled above her.

With his knee he spread her legs, positioned himself above her. "You're sure?"

What was he waiting for?

She arched her hips, taking him inside, then moaned at the sweet stretching pleasure.

That was what she had been wanting for a very long time.

Breathing hard, Lance fell back against the bed.

She'd been amazing.

Beautiful, fun, witty, sexy, actively participating in their mating, urging him on, telling him what she wanted, what she needed. Showing him.

The chemistry between them was unparalleled. Never had he experienced anything like what they'd just shared.

"That. Was. Amazing."

He grinned at her punctuated words. "My thoughts exactly."

He turned onto his side and stared at her. "You are amazing."

"Ha. Wasn't me."

"I think it was."

"Right. I assure you that I've been there every time I've had sex in the past and it's never been like that so it must be you who is amazing."

His insides warmed at her admission. "For the record, it's never been like that for me either."

Her expression pinched and she scooted up on a pillow.

Shaking her head, she went for the sheet that was bunched up at the foot of the bed. When she'd covered her beautiful body, she turned to him.

"I don't really think I need to say this, not with a man like you, but I'm going to, just in case. I don't want there to be any confusion."

He knew from her words, her tone what she was going to say. He was glad. He felt the same, but hearing the reminder was good and perhaps needed.

"Despite your amazing orgasm-giving ability, I'm not looking for a long-term relationship."

"Me, either," he assured her, trying not to let his ego get too big at her praise.

"I guess that's crude of me, to talk about the end when we're still in bed and I feel wonderful. But we work together so we need to be clear about the boundaries of our relationship so work doesn't become messy."

The thought of ending things with her, not being able to touch her, kiss her, make love to her and experience what they'd just shared, because it might make things messy, wasn't a pleasant thought, but it should be.

He didn't want marriage or kids, didn't want that responsibility, that weight on his heart, that replacing of Shelby. He'd made a vow to his first love. He owed Shelby his heart and more. McKenzie was right to remind them both of the guidelines they'd agreed to. Setting an end date and clear boundaries was a smart move.

Two months for them to enjoy each other's bodies, then move on with their lives. Him with his main focus being his career and charity work in memory of Shelby. McKenzie with her career and her running and whatever else filled her life with joy.

Two months and they'd call it quits. That sounded just right to him.

* * *

Staring at the oh-so-hot naked man in her bed, McKenzie hugged the sheet tighter to her.

Please agree with me, she silently pleaded.

She'd just had the best sex of her life and couldn't fathom the idea of not repeating the magic she'd just experienced.

But she would do just that if he didn't agree.

Already she was risking too much. That's why she usually ended her relationships after a month, because she didn't want pesky emotional attachments that might lead her down the paths her parents had taken. She didn't want a future that held multiple marriages and multiple divorces like her father. Neither did she want the whiny, miserable, man-needing life her mother led.

Bachelorettehood was the life for her, all the way.

Hearing Lance agree that they'd end things in two months was important, necessary for them to carry on. She simply wouldn't risk anything longer. Already she was giving him double the time she usually spent with a man.

He deserved double time.

Triple time.

Forever.

No, not forever. She didn't do forever. Two months, then adios, even if he was an orgasm-giving god.

"Promise me," she urged, desperately needing the words.

"Two months sounds perfect."

Relief flooded her, because she hadn't wanted to tell him to leave. For two months she didn't have to.

CHAPTER TEN

"You can't be working the entire Christmas holiday," Lance insisted, following McKenzie to the hospital cafeteria table where she put down her food tray.

She'd gotten a chicken salad croissant and a side salad. He'd gone for a more hearty meal, but had ended up grabbing a croissant as well.

Sitting down at the table, she glanced at him. "I'm not, but I am working at the clinic half a day on Christmas Eve and then working half a day in the emergency room on Christmas morning." She'd done so the past few years so the regular emergency room doctor could have the morning off with his kids and she liked filling in from time to time so she kept her emergency care skills sharp.

"When will you celebrate with your parents?"

Bile rose up in her throat at the thought of introducing Lance to her parents. Her mother would probably hit on him and her dad would probably ask him what he thought about wife number five's plastic surgeon–constructed chest. No, she wouldn't be taking Lance home for the holidays.

Actually, when she'd talked to her mother a few days ago, Violet had said she was going to her sister's for a few days and spending the holidays with her family. She hadn't mentioned Beau, the latest live-in boyfriend, so McKenzie wasn't sure if Beau was going, staying or if he was history. Her father had planned a ski trip in Vermont with his bride and a group of their friends.

"We don't celebrate the holidays like other folks."

"How's that?"

"We'll meet up at some point in January and have dinner or something. We just don't make a big deal of the day. It's way too commercialized anyway, you know."

"This coming from the winner of the best costume in the Christmas parade."

She couldn't quite keep her smile hidden. The call from the mayor telling her she'd won the award had surprised her, as had the Christmas ornament he'd dropped by the clinic to commemorate her honor.

"Cecilia is the one who should get all the kudos for that. She put my costume together."

"But you wore it so well," he assured her, giving her a once-over. "You wear that lab coat nicely, too, Dr. Sanders."

She arched a brow at him and gave a mock-condescending shake of her head. "You hitting on me, Dr. Spencer?"

"With a baseball bat."

She rolled her eyes. "Men, always talking about size."

He laughed.

"Speaking of size, you should see the tree my mother put up in her family room. I swear she searches for the biggest one on the lot every year and that's her sole criterion for buying."

"She puts up a live tree?"

"She puts up a slew of trees. All are artificial except the one in the family room. There, she goes all out and insists on a real tree. There's a row of evergreens behind my parents' house, marking Christmases past."

McKenzie couldn't even recall the last Christmas tree her mother had put up. Maybe a skimpy tinsel one that had seen better days when McKenzie had still been young enough to ask about Santa and Christmas. Violet had never been much of a holiday person, especially not after McKenzie's father had left.

"She wants to meet you."

McKenzie's brow arched. "Why would she want to do that? For that matter, how does she even know about me?"

"She asked if I was seeing anyone and I told her about you."

Talking to his mother about her just seemed wrong.

"She shouldn't meet me."

"Why not?"

"Mothers should only meet significant others who have the potential for being around for a while."

"Look, telling her I was dating someone was easier than showing up and there being some single female there eager to meet me and plan our future together. It's really not as big a deal as you're making it for you to come to my parents' at Christmas."

Maybe not to him, but the thought of meeting his family was a very big deal to her. She didn't meet families. That implied things that just weren't true.

"Obviously you haven't been paying attention," she pointed out. "I'll be here on Christmas, working."

"The shifts are abbreviated on the holidays. What time will you get off?"

"Oh, no. You're not trapping me that way."

He gave her an innocent look. "What way?"

"The way that whatever time I say you're going to say, 'Oh, that's perfect. Just come on over when you're finished.'"

"Hey, McKenzie?"

She frowned at him, knowing what he was about to say.

"The time you get off from the emergency room is perfect. Just come to my parents' house when you're finished."

"Meeting parents implies a commitment you and I don't have," she reiterated.

"There'll be lots of people there. Aunts. Uncles. Cousins. People even I've never met. It's a party. You'll have fun and it's really not a big deal, except it saves me from my mother trying to set me up with every single nonrelated female she knows."

How in the world had he talked her into this? McKenzie asked herself crossly as she pushed the Spencers' doorbell.

She didn't do this.

Only, apparently, this year she did.

Even to the point she'd made a dessert to bring with her to Lance's parents. How corny was that?

She shouldn't be here. She didn't do "meet the parents." She just didn't.

Panic set in. She turned, determined to escape before anyone knew she was there.

At that moment the front door opened.

"You're here."

"Not really," she countered. "Forget you saw me. I'm out of here."

Shaking his head, he grinned. "Get in here."

"I think I made a mistake."

His brows rose. "McKenzie, you just drove almost an hour to get here and not so you could get here and leave without Christmas dinner."

"I've done crazier things." Like agree to come to Christmas dinner with Lance's family in the first place.

"Did you make something?" He gestured to the dish she held.

"A dessert, but—"

"No buts, McKenzie. Get in here."

She took a deep breath. He was right. She was being ridiculous. She had gotten off work, gone home, showered, grabbed the dessert she'd made the night before and typed his parents' address into her GPS.

And driven almost an hour to get here.

"Fine, but you owe me."

He leaned forward, kissed the tip of her nose. "Anything you want."

"Promises. Promises."

He grinned, took the dish from her, and motioned her inside. "I'm glad you're here. I was afraid you'd change your mind."

"I did," she reminded him as she stepped into his parents' foyer. "Only I waited a bit too late because you caught me before I could escape."

"Then I'm glad I noticed your headlights as your car pulled into the driveway, because I missed you last night."

He'd driven to his parents' home the afternoon before when he'd finished seeing his patients. It had been the first evening since their frozen yogurt date that they'd not seen each other.

She'd missed him too.

Which didn't jibe well, but she didn't have time to think too much on it, because a pretty woman who appeared to be much younger than McKenzie knew she had to be stepped into the foyer. She had sparkly blue eyes, dark brown hair that she had clipped up, black slacks and the prettiest Christmas sweater McKenzie had ever seen. Her smile lit up her entire face.

Lance looked a lot like his mother.

"We are so glad you're here!" she exclaimed, her Southern drawl so pronounced it was almost like something off a television show. "Lance has been useless for the past hour, waiting on you to get here."

"Thanks, Mom. You just called me useless to my girl." Lance's tone was teasing, his look toward his mother full of adoration.

McKenzie wanted to go on record that she wasn't Lance's girl, but technically she supposed she was. At least for the time being.

"Nonsense. She knows what I meant," his mother dismissed his claim and pulled McKenzie into a tight hug. She smelled of cinnamon and cookies.

Christmas, McKenzie thought. His mother smelled of Christmas. Not McKenzie's past Christmases, but the way Christmas was supposed to smell. Warm, inviting, full of goodness and happiness.

"It's nice to meet you," McKenzie said, not quite sure what to make of her hug. Lance's mother's hug had been real, warm, welcoming. She couldn't recall the last time her own mother or father had given her such a hug. Had they ever?

"Not nearly as nice as it is to finally meet one of Lance's girlfriends."

Did he not usually bring his girlfriends home? He'd said her being there was no big deal. If he didn't usually bring anyone home, then her presence was a big deal. She wanted to ask, but decided it wasn't her place because really what did it matter? She was here now. Whatever he'd done with his past girlfriends didn't apply to her, just as what he did with her wouldn't apply to his future girlfriends.

Future girlfriends. Ugh. She didn't like the thought of him with anyone but her. His smile, his touch, his kisses, they belonged to her. At least for now, she reminded herself.

"I'm glad you're here." Lance leaned in, kissed her briefly on the mouth, then took her hand. "I hope you came hungry."

Her gaze cut to Lance's and she wondered if he'd read her thoughts again?

"Take a deep breath. It's time to meet the rest of the crew," he warned.

"Be nice, Lance. You'll scare her off. They aren't that bad and you know it," his mother scolded.

Lance just winked at her.

Two hours later, McKenzie had to agree with Lance's mother. His family wasn't that bad. She'd met his grandparents, who were so hard of hearing they had everyone talking loudly so they could keep up with the conversation, his aunts and uncles, his cousins, and a handful of children who belonged to his cousins.

It was quite a bunch: loud, talking over one another, laughing, eating and truly enjoying each other's company.

The kids seemed to adore Lance. They called him Uncle Lance, although technically he was their second cousin.

"You're quiet," Lance observed, leaning in close so that his words were just for her ears.

"Just taking it all in," she admitted.

"We're something else, for sure. Is this similar to your family get-togethers?"

McKenzie laughed. "Not even close."

"How so?"

"I won't bore you with my childhood woes."

"Nothing about you would bore me, McKenzie. I want to know more about you."

She started to ask what would be the point, but somehow that comment felt wrong in this loving, warm environment, so she picked up her glass of tea, took a sip, then whispered, "I'll tell you some other time."

That seemed to appease him. They finished eating. Everyone, men and women, helped clear the table. The kids had eaten at a couple of card tables set up in the kitchen and they too cleared their spots without prompting. McKenzie was amazed at how they all seemed to work together so cohesively.

The men then retired to the large family room while

the women put away leftovers and loaded the dishwasher. All except Lance. He seemed reluctant to leave McKenzie.

"I'll be fine. I'm sure they won't bite."

He still looked hesitant.

"Seriously, what's the worst that could happen?"

What indeed? Lance wondered. He had rarely brought women home and never to a Christmas function. His entire family had been teasing him that this must be the one for him to bring her home to Christmas with the family. He'd tried to explain that he and McKenzie had been co-workers and friends for years, but the more he'd talked, the more he reminded them that he'd already met and lost "the one," the more they'd smiled. By the time McKenzie arrived, he'd been half-afraid his family would have them walking down the aisle before morning.

He didn't think she'd appreciate any implication that they were more than just a casual couple.

They weren't. Just a hot and heavy two-month relationship destined to go nowhere because McKenzie didn't do long-term commitment and his seventeen-year-old self had vowed to always love Shelby, for his heart to always be loyal to her memory.

What was the worst that could happen? He hesitated.

"Seriously, Lance. I'm a big girl. They aren't going to scare me off."

"I just…" He knew he was being ridiculous. "I don't mind helping clean up."

"Lance Donovan Spencer, go visit with your grandparents. You've not seen them since Thanksgiving," his mother ordered. "That will give me and your girl time to get to know each other without you looming over us."

"Looming?" he protested indignantly.

"Go." His mother pointed toward the door.

Lance laughed. "I can tell my presence and help is not

appreciated or wanted around here, so I will go visit with my grandmother who loves me very much."

"Hmm, maybe she's who you should list on your references," McKenzie teased him, her eyes twinkling.

"Maybe. Mom's been bumped right off."

"I heard that," his mom called out over her shoulder.

He leaned in and kissed McKenzie's cheek. "I'm right in the next room if their interrogation gets to be too much."

"Noted." McKenzie was smiling, like she wouldn't mind his mother's, aunts' and cousins' questions. Lord, he hoped not. They didn't have boundaries and McKenzie had boundaries that made the Great Wall of China look like a playpen.

"Lance tells me you two have only been dating for a few weeks," his mother said moments after Lance left the kitchen.

"You know he's never brought a woman home for Christmas before, right?" This came from one of Lance's cousins' wives, Sara Beth.

"He seems to be head over heels about you," another said. "Told us you two work together and recently became an item."

"We want the full scoop," one of his dad's sisters added.

"Um, well, sounds like you already know the full scoop," McKenzie began slowly. She didn't want to give Lance's family the wrong idea. "We have been friends since I returned to Coopersville after finishing my residency."

"So you're from Coopersville originally? Your family is still there?"

"My mother is. My dad lives here in Lewisburg."

His mother's eyes lit up with excitement. "We might know him. What's his name?"

She hoped they didn't know him. Okay, so he was a highly successful lawyer, but personally? Her father was a mess. A horrible, womanizing, cheating mess. If Lance's mother knew him, it probably meant he'd hit on her. Not the impression McKenzie wanted Lance's mother to have of her.

Avoiding the question, she said instead, "I don't have any brothers or sisters but, like Lance, I do have a few cousins." Nice enough people but they rarely all got together. Really, the only time McKenzie saw them was when one of them was sick and was seen at the clinic. "My parents divorced when I was four and I never quite got past that."

She only added the last part so Lance's family would hopefully move on past the subject of her parents. Definitely not because she wanted to talk about her parents' divorce. She never talked about that. At least, not the nitty-gritty details that had led up to her world falling apart.

"Poor thing," Lance's mother sympathized. "Divorce is hard at any age."

"Amen," another of Lance's aunts said. "Lance's Uncle Gerry is my second husband. The first and I were like gasoline and fire, always explosive."

The conversation continued while they cleaned up the remainder of the dishes and food, jumping from one subject to another but never back to McKenzie's parents. She liked Lance's noisy, warm family.

"Well, we're just so happy you're here, McKenzie. It's about time that boy found someone to pull him out of the past."

McKenzie glanced toward the aunt who'd spoken up. Her confusion must have shown because the women looked back and forth at each other as if trying to decide how much more to say.

Sara Beth gave McKenzie an empathetic look. "I guess he never told you about Shelby?"

Who was Shelby and what had she meant to Lance? "No."

The woman winced as if she wished she could erase

having mentioned the woman's name. "Shelby was Lance's first love."

Was. An ominous foreboding took hold of McKenzie.

"What happened?"

"She died." This came from Sara Beth. Every pair of eyes in the room was trained on McKenzie to gauge her reaction, triggering the usual reaction to being stared at that she always had.

Lance's first love had died and he'd never breathed a word.

"Enough talk about the past and anything but how wonderful it is to have McKenzie with us," Lance's mother dried her hands on a towel and pulled McKenzie over to the counter for another of her tight, all-encompassing hugs. "Truly, we are grateful that you are in my son's life. He is a special man with a big heart and you are a fortunate young woman."

"Yes," McKenzie agreed, stunned at the thought someone Lance had loved had died. Was he still in love with Shelby? How had the woman died? How long ago? "Yes, he is a special man."

CHAPTER ELEVEN

"YOU SURE ABOUT THIS?" McKenzie asked the man stretching out beside her. He wore dark running pants that emphasized his calf and thigh muscles and a bright-colored long-sleeved running shirt that outlined a chest McKenzie had taken great pleasure in exploring the night before as they'd lain in bed and "rung in" the New Year.

Lance glanced at her and grinned. "I'll be waiting for you at the finish line."

She hoped so. She hoped Lance hadn't been teasing about being a runner. He was in great shape, had phenomenal endurance, but she'd still never known him to run. But the truth was he hadn't stayed the whole night at her place ever, so he could do the same as her and run in the early morning before work. They had sex, often lay in bed talking and touching lightly afterward, then he went home. Just as he had the night before. She hadn't asked him to stay. He hadn't asked to. Just, each night, whenever he got ready to go, he kissed her good-night and left.

Truth was, she'd have let him stay Christmas night after they'd got back from his parents'. He'd insisted on following her back to her place. Despite the late hour, he'd come in, held her close, then left. She hadn't wanted him to go. She'd have let him stay every night since. He just hadn't wanted to. Or, if he had wanted to, he'd chosen to go home anyway.

Why was that? Did it have to do with Shelby? Should she tell him that she knew about his first love? That his family had told her about his loss? They just hadn't told her any of the details surrounding the mysterious woman Lance had loved.

Maybe the details didn't matter. They shouldn't matter.

Only McKenzie admitted they did. Perhaps it was just curiosity. Perhaps it was jealousy. Perhaps it was something more she couldn't put her finger on.

She'd almost asked him about Shelby a dozen times, but always changed her mind. If he wanted her to know, he'd tell her.

Today was the first day of a new year. A new beginning. Who knew, maybe tonight he'd stay.

If not, she was okay with that, too. He might be right in going, in not adding sleeping together to their relationship, because she didn't count the light dozing they sometimes did after their still phenomenal comings together as sleep. Sleeping together until morning would be another whole level of intimacy.

"You don't have to try to run next to me," she advised, thinking they were intimate enough already. Too intimate because imagining life without him was already becoming difficult. Maybe they could stay close friends after their two months were up. Maybe. "Just keep your own steady pace and I'll keep mine. We'll meet up at the end."

Grinning, he nodded. "Yes, ma'am. I'll keep that in mind."

They continued to stretch their muscles as the announcer talked, telling them about the cause they were running for, about the rules, etc. Soon they were off.

McKenzie never tried to take the lead early on. In some races she never took the lead. Not that she didn't always do her best, but sometimes there were just faster runners for that particular distance. Today she expected to do well, but perhaps not win as she was much more of an endurance runner than a speed one.

Lance ran beside her and to her pleased surprise he didn't try to talk. In the past when she'd convinced friends to run with her, they'd wanted to have a gab session. That was until they became so breathless they stopped to walk, and then they often expected her to stop and walk with them.

McKenzie ran.

Lance easily kept pace with her. Halfway in she began to wonder if she was slowing him down rather than the other way around. She picked up her pace, pushing herself, suddenly wanting distance between them. Without any huffing or puffing he ran along beside her as if she hadn't just upped their pace. That annoyed her.

"You've been holding out on me," she accused a little breathily, thinking it was bad when she was the one reverting to talking. Next thing you knew she'd be stopping to walk.

"Me?" His gaze cut to her. "I told you that I ran."

"I've never seen you at any of the local runs and yet clearly you do run."

"I don't do organized runs or competitions."

Didn't do organized runs or competitions? McKenzie frowned. What kind of an answer was that when he clearly enjoyed running as much as she did? Well, maybe almost as much.

"That's hard to believe with the way you're into every charity in the region," she said. "Why wouldn't you participate in these fund-raisers when they're an easy way to raise money for great causes? For that matter, why aren't you organizing races to raise money for all your special causes?"

McKenzie was a little too smart for her own good. Lance was involved with a large number of charities and helped support many others, but never those that had to do with running.

He did run several times a week, but always alone, always to clear his head, always with someone else at his side, mentally if not physically.

High school cross-country had been where he'd first met Shelby. She'd been a year older than him and had had a different set of friends, so although he'd seen the pretty brunette around school he hadn't known her. She'd have been better off if he never had.

"No one can do everything," he answered McKenzie.

"I'm beginning to think you do."

"Not even close. You and I just happen to have a lot in common. We enjoy the same things."

She shook her head. "Nope. I don't enjoy singing."

"I think you would if you'd relax."

"Standing onstage, with people looking at me?" She cut her gaze to him. "Never going to happen."

Keeping his pace matched to hers, he glanced at her. "You don't like things that make people look at you, do you, McKenzie?"

"Nope."

"Because of your parents?"

"I may not have mentioned this before, but I don't like talking while I run. I'm a silent runner."

He chuckled. "That a hint for me to be quiet?"

"You catch on quick."

They kept up the more intense pace until they crossed the finish line. The last few minutes of the race Lance debated on whether or not to let McKenzie cross the finish line first. Ultimately, he decided she wasn't the kind of woman who'd appreciate a man letting her win.

In the last stretch he increased his speed. So did McKenzie. If he hadn't been a bit winded, he'd have laughed at her competitive spirit. Instead, he ran.

So did she.

They crossed the finish line together. The judge declared Lance the winner by a fraction of a second, but Lance would have just as easily have believed that McKenzie had crossed first.

She was doubled over, gasping for air. His own lungs couldn't suck in enough air either. He walked around, slowly catching his breath. When he turned back, she was glaring.

"You were holding out on me," she accused breathlessly, her eyes narrowed.

"Huh?"

"You were considering letting me win." Her words came out a little choppy between gasps for air.

"In case you didn't notice…" he sucked in a deep gulp of air "… I was trying to cross that finish line first."

"You were sandbagging."

He laughed. "Sandbagging?"

"How long have you been running?"

"Since high school." Not that he wanted to talk about it. He didn't. Talking about this particular subject might lead to questions he didn't want to answer.

"You competed?"

He nodded.

"Me, too." She straightened, fully expanding her lungs with air. "I did my undergraduate studies on a track scholarship."

Despite the memories assailing him, the corners of Lance's mouth tugged upward. "Something else we have in common."

McKenzie just looked at him, then rolled her eyes. "We don't have that much in common."

"More than you seem to want to acknowledge."

"Maybe," she conceded. "Let's go congratulate the guy who beat us both. He lives about thirty minutes from here.

His time is usually about twenty to thirty seconds better than mine. He usually only competes in the five-kilometer races, though. Nothing shorter, nothing longer."

They congratulated the winner, hung out around the tent, rehydrating, got their second and third place medals, then headed toward McKenzie's house.

They showered together then, a long time later, got ready to go and eat.

The first day of the New Year turned into the first week, then the first month.

McKenzie began to feel panicky, knowing her time with Lance was coming to an end as the one-month mark came and went. Each day following passed like sand swiftly falling through an hourglass.

Then she realized that the day before Valentine's Day marked the end of the two months she'd promised him. Seriously, the day before Valentine's?

Why did that even matter? She'd never cared if she had a significant other on that hyped-up holiday in the past. Most years she'd been in a casual relationship and she'd gotten a box of chocolates and flowers and had given a funny card to her date for the evening. Why should this year feel different? Why did the idea of chocolates and flowers from Lance seem as if it would be different from gifts she'd received in the past? Why did the idea of giving him a card seem to fall short?

She'd be ending things with Lance the day before every other couple would be celebrating their love.

She and Lance weren't in love. She wasn't sure love even truly existed.

A vision of Lance's grandparents, married for sixty years, his parents, married for forty years, ran through her mind and she had to reconsider. Maybe love did exist, but not for anyone with her genetic makeup. Already her dad was complaining about his new wife and had flirted outrageously with their waitress when they'd had their usual belated Christmas dinner a few weeks back. Hearing that his new marriage would be ending soon wouldn't surprise McKenzie in the slightest. Her mother, well, her mother had taken up the vegan life because Beau was history and her new "'love" was all about living green. Her mother was even planning to plant out her own garden this spring and wanted to know if McKenzie had any requests.

McKenzie had no issue with her mother trying to live more healthily. She was glad of it, even. But the woman enjoyed nothing more than a big juicy steak, which was what she ordered on the rare occasions she met McKenzie for a meal—usually in between boyfriends or at Christmas or birthdays.

McKenzie had managed both meals with her parents this year without Lance joining them. Fortunately, his volunteer work oftentimes had him busy immediately following work and she had scheduled both meals with her parents on evenings he had Celebration Graduation meetings.

"You've been staring at your screen for the past ten minutes," Lance pointed out, gesturing to her idle laptop. "Problem patient?"

He'd come over, brought their dinner with him, and they'd been sitting on her sofa, remotely logged in to their work laptops and charting their day's patients while watching a reality television program.

McKenzie hit a button, saving her work, then turned to him. "My mind just isn't on this tonight."

"I noticed." He saved his own work, set his laptop down on her coffee table and turned to her. "What's up?"

"I was just thinking about Valentine's Day."

His smile spread across his face and lit up his eyes. "Making plans for how you're going to surprise me with a lacy red number and high heels?" He waggled his brows suggestively.

Despite knowing he was mostly teasing, she shook her head. "We won't be together on Valentine's Day. Our two months is up the day before. The end is near."

His smile faded and his forehead wrinkled. "There's no reason we shouldn't be able to spend Valentine's Day together. I have the Celebration Graduation Valentine's Day dance at the high school that I'll be helping to chaperone. It ends at ten and it'll take me another twenty to thirty minutes to help clean up. But we can still do something, then we'll call it quits after that."

She shook her head. "You already had plans for that evening. That's good."

She, however, did not and would be acutely aware of his absence from her life, and not just because of the holiday.

"I hadn't really thought about it being the end of our two months. You could volunteer at the dance with me."

She shook her head again. "Not a good idea."

"Think you'd be a bad influence on those high schoolers?" Even though his tone was teasing, his eyes searched hers.

"I probably would," she agreed, just to avoid a discussion of the truth. They would be finished the night before. There would be no more charting together, dining together, going to dances or parties together, no more running together, as they'd started doing every morning at four. Lance would be gone, would meet someone else, would date them, and, despite what he claimed, he would very likely eventually find whatever he was looking for in a woman and marry her.

Was he looking for someone like Shelby?

What was Shelby like?

Why had he still not mentioned the woman to her?

Then again, why would he mention her? He and McKenzie were temporary. He owed her nothing, no explanation of his past relationships, no explanation of his future plans.

Yet there were things about him she wanted to know. Suddenly needed to know.

"Do you want kids?" Why she asked the question she wasn't sure. It wasn't as if the answer mattered to her or was even applicable. She and Lance had no future together.

To her surprise, he shook his head. "I have no plans to ever have children."

Recalling how great he was with his cousins' kids, that shocked her. Then again, had she asked him the question because she'd expected a different answer? That she'd expected him to say he planned to have an entire houseful, and that way she could have used that information as one more thing to put between them because, with her genetics, no way could she ever have children.

"You'd make a fantastic dad."

His brow lifted and he regarded her for a few long moments before asking, "You pregnant, McKenzie?"

Her mouth fell open and she squished up her nose. "Absolutely not."

"You sure? You've not had a menstrual cycle since we've been together. I hadn't really thought about it until just now, but I should have."

Her face heated at his comment. They were doctors, so it was ridiculous that she was blushing. But at this moment she was a woman and he was a man. Medicine had nothing to do with their conversation. This was personal. Too personal.

"I rarely have my cycle. My gynecologist says it's because I run so much and don't retain enough body fat for proper estrogen storage. It's highly unlikely that I'd get pregnant. But even if that weren't an issue," she reminded him, "you've used a condom every single time we've had sex. I can't be pregnant."

Not once had she even considered that as a possibility. Truth was, she questioned if her body would even allow her to get pregnant if she wanted to, which she didn't. No way would she want to bring a baby in to the world the way her parents had.

"Stranger things have happened."

"Than my getting pregnant?" She shook her head in denial. "That would be the strangest ever. I'm not meant to have children."

His curiosity was obviously piqued as he studied her. "Why not?"

"Bad genetics."

"Your parents are ill?"

How was she supposed to answer that one? With the truth, probably. She took a deep breath.

"Physically, they are as healthy as can be. Mentally and emotionally, they are messed up."

"Depression?"

"My mother suffers from depression. Maybe my dad, too, really. They both have made horrible life choices that they are now stuck living with."

"Your dad is a lawyer?"

She nodded.

"What does your mom do?"

"Whatever the man currently in her life tells her to do."

Lance seemed to let that sink in for a few moments. "She's remarried?"

McKenzie shook her head. "She's never remarried. I think she purposely stays single because my father has to pay her alimony until she remarries or dies."

"Your father is remarried, though?"

"At the moment, but ask me again in a month and who knows what the answer will be."

"How many times has he remarried?"

She didn't want to answer, shouldn't have let this conversation even start. She should have finished her charts, not opened up an emotional can of worms that led to conversations about her menstrual cycle, pregnancy and her parents. What had she been thinking?

"McKenzie?"

"He's on his fifth marriage."

Lance winced. "Hard to find the one, eh?"

"Oh, he finds them all right. In all the wrong places. He's not known for his faithfulness. My guess is that he's to blame for all his failed marriages. Definitely he was with his and my mother's."

"There's always two sides to every story."

"My mother and I walked in on him in his office with his secretary."

"As in…"

Feeling sick at her stomach, McKenzie nodded. She'd never said those words out loud. Not ever. Cecilia knew, but not because McKenzie had told her the details, just that she'd figured it out from overheard arguments between McKenzie's parents.

"How old were you?"

"Four."

CHAPTER TWELVE

LANCE TRIED TO imagine how a four-year-old would react to walking in on her father in a compromising situation with a woman who wasn't her mother. He couldn't imagine it. His own family took commitment seriously. When they gave their word, their heart to another they meant it.

His own heart squeezed. Hadn't he given his word to Shelby? Hadn't he promised to love her forever? To not ever forget the young girl who'd taught him what it meant to care for another, who'd brought him from boyhood to manhood?

He had. He did. He would. Forever.

He owed her so much.

"That must have been traumatic," he mused, not knowing exactly what to say but wanting to comfort McKenzie all the same. Wanting not to think of Shelby right now. Lately he'd not wanted to think of her a lot, and had resented how much he thought of her, of how guilty he felt that he didn't want to think of her anymore.

How could he not want to think of her when it was his fault she was no longer living the life she had been meant to live? When if it wasn't for him she'd be a doctor? Be making a difference in so many people's lives?

"It wasn't the first time he'd cheated."

Lance stared at McKenzie's pale face. "How do you know?"

"My mother launched herself at them, screaming and yelling and clawing and...well, you get the idea. She said some pretty choice things that my father didn't deny."

"You were only four," he reminded her, trying to en-vision the scene from a four-year-old's perspective and shuttering on the inside at the horror. "Maybe you mis-understood."

She shook her head. "He doesn't deserve you or any-one else defending him. He doesn't even bother defend-ing himself anymore. Just says it's genetic and he can't help himself."

"Bull."

That had McKenzie's head shooting up. "What?"

"Bull. If he really loved someone else more than he loved himself then being faithful wouldn't be an issue. It would be easy, what came naturally from that love."

McKenzie took a deep breath. "Then maybe that's the problem. No one has ever been able to compete with his own self-love. Not my mother, not his other wives or girl-friends and certainly not me."

There was a depth of pain in her voice that made Lance's heart ache for her. "Did he have more children?"

McKenzie shook her head. "He had a vasectomy so that mistake would never happen again."

"Implying that you were a mistake?"

McKenzie shrugged.

"He's a fool, McKenzie. A stupid, selfish fool."

"Agreed." She brushed her hands over her thighs then stood. "I'm going to get a drink of water. You need any-thing?"

"Just you."

She paused. "Sorry, but the discussion about my parents has killed any possibility of that for some time."

"Not what I meant."

She stared down at him. "Then what did you mean?"

Good question. What had he meant?

That he needed her?

Physically? They were powerful in bed together. But it was more than sex. Mentally, she challenged him with her quick intelligence and wit. Emotionally...emotionally she had him a tangled-up mess. A tangled-up mess he had no right to be feeling.

He'd asked her to give him two months. That's all she planned to give him, that's all he'd thought he'd wanted from McKenzie.

Usually he had long-lasting relationships even though he knew they were never going anywhere. He'd always been up-front with whomever he'd been dating on that point. When things came to an end, he'd always been okay with it, his heart not really involved.

With McKenzie he'd wanted that time limit as much as she had, because everything had felt different right from the start.

She made him question everything.

The past. The present. The future. What had always seemed so clear was now a blurred unknown.

That they had planned a definite ending was a good thing, the best thing. He had a vow to keep. Guilt mingled in with whatever else was going on. Horrible, horrible guilt that would lie heavily on his shoulders for the rest of his life.

"I'll take that glass of water after all," he said in way of an answer to her question. Not that it was an answer, but it was all he knew to say.

"Yeah, this conversation has left a bad taste in both our mouths."

Something like that.

"Edith came in to see me this morning."

Lance glanced up from his desk. "How is she doing?"

McKenzie sank down in the chair across from his desk.

"Quite well, really. She had a long list of complaints, of course. But overall she looked good and the latest imaging of her chest shows that her pulmonary embolism has resolved."

"That's fantastic. She's a feisty thing."

"That she is."

He studied her a moment then set down the pen he held, walked around his desk, shut his office door, then wrapped his arms around her.

"What are you doing?"

"Shh..." he told her. "Don't say anything."

Not that his arms didn't feel amazing, but she frowned up at him. "Don't tell me what to do."

He chuckled. "You're such a stubborn woman."

"You're just now figuring that out, Mr. Persistence?"

"No, I knew that going in."

"And?"

"I can appreciate that fact about you even if it drives me crazy at times."

"Such as now?"

He shook his head. "Not really because for all your protesting, you are still letting me hold you."

"Why are you holding me? I thought we agreed we wouldn't do this at work? You promised me we wouldn't."

"This is a hug between friends. A means of offering comfort and support. I never promised not to give you those things when you obviously need a hug."

"Oh." Because really what could she say to that? He was right. She obviously had needed a hug. His hug.

Only being in his arms, her body pressed close to his, her nostrils filled with his spicy clean scent, made her aware of all the other things she needed him for, too.

Things she didn't need to be distracted by at work.

She pulled from his arms and he let her go.

"Sorry I bothered you. I just wanted to let you know about Edith and that I'd be at the hospital during lunch."

"I'll see you there."

"But—"

"I'll see you there," he repeated.

"You're a persistent man, Lance."

"You're a stubborn woman, McKenzie."

A smile tugged at her lips. "Fine, I'll see you at the hospital at lunch."

Lance had a Celebration Graduation meeting for last-minute Valentine's Day dance planning that he'd tried to convince McKenzie to attend with him. She didn't want to get too involved in his pet projects because their days together as a couple were dwindling. The more entangled their lives were the more difficult saying goodbye was going to be.

McKenzie's phone rang and she almost didn't answer when she saw that it was her mother. When she heard what her mother had to say she wished she hadn't.

"I'm getting married."

Three little words that had McKenzie dropping everything and agreeing to meet her mother at her house.

Violet's house was the same house where McKenzie had grown up. McKenzie's father had paid for the house where they'd lived when he'd first been starting his law career. He'd also provided a monthly check that had apparently abdicated him of all other obligations to his daughter.

"Whatever is going through your head?" McKenzie asked the moment she walked into her mother's living room. She came to a halt when she saw the man sitting on her mother's sofa. The one who was much younger than her mother. "How old are you?"

"What does it matter how old he is?" her mother interrupted. "Age is only a number."

"Mom, if I'm older than him, I'm walking out of this house right now."

Her mother glanced at the man and giggled. *Giggled.* "He's eight years older than you, McKenzie."

"Which means he's ten years younger than you," McKenzie reminded her. She wasn't a prude, didn't think relationships should be bound by age, except for when it came to her mother. Her mother dating a man so much younger just didn't sit well.

"Yes, I am a lucky woman that Yves has fallen for me in my old, decrepit state," her mother remarked wryly. "Thank goodness I'll have him around to help me with my walker and picking out a nursing home."

"Mom…" McKenzie began, then glanced back and forth between her mother and the man she was apparently engaged to. She sank down onto her mother's sofa. "So, maybe you should tell me more about this whole getting-married bit since I know for a fact you were single at the beginning of the year."

She was used to her father marrying on a whim, but her mother had been single since the day she'd divorced McKenzie's father almost three decades ago. Violet dated and chased men, but she didn't marry.

"I met Yves at a New Year's Eve party."

"You met him just over a month ago. Don't you think it's a little quick to be getting engaged?"

"Getting married," her mother corrected, holding out her hand to show McKenzie the ring on her finger. "We're already engaged."

The stone wasn't a diamond, but was a pretty emerald that matched the color of her mother's eyes perfectly.

"When is the wedding supposed to take place?"

"Valentine's Day."

Valentine's Day. The first day McKenzie would be without Lance and her mother was walking down the aisle.

She regarded her mother. "You're sure about this?"

"Positive."

"Why now? After all this time, why would you choose to marry again?"

"The only reason I've not remarried all these years is because I hadn't met the right person, McKenzie. I have had other proposals over the years, I just haven't wanted to say yes until Yves."

Other proposals? McKenzie hadn't known. Still, her mother. Married.

"Does Dad know?"

"What does it matter if your father knows that I'm going to remarry? He has nothing to do with my life."

"Mom, if you remarry Dad will quit sending you a check every month. How are you going to get by?"

"I'll take care of her," Yves popped up, moving to stand protectively by Violet.

"And how are you going to do that?"

"I run a health-food store on the square."

McKenzie had read about a new store opening on the square, had been planning to swing by to check out what they had.

"He more than runs it," Violet bragged. "He owns the store. Plus, he has two others that are already successful in towns nearby."

So maybe the guy wasn't after her mother for a free ride.

"You know I don't need your permission to get married, McKenzie."

"I know that, Mother."

"But I had hoped you'd be happy for me."

McKenzie cringed on the inside. How was she supposed to be happy for her mother when she worried that her mother was just going to be hurt yet again? She'd seen her devastation all those years ago, had watched the depression take hold and not let go for years. Why would she want her mother to risk that again? Especially with a man so much younger than she was?

She must have asked the last question out loud because her mother beamed at Yves, placed her hand in his and answered, "Because for the first time in a long time, maybe ever, I know what it feels like to be loved. It's a wonderful feeling, McKenzie. I hope that someday you know exactly what I mean."

Lance hit McKenzie's number for what had to be the dozenth time. Why wasn't she answering her phone?

He'd driven out to her place, but she wasn't home. Where would she be? Cecilia's perhaps? He'd drive out there, too, but that made him feel a little too desperate.

Unfortunately, he was the bearer of bad news regarding a patient she'd sent to the emergency room earlier. The man had been in the midst of a heart attack and had been airlifted to Atlanta. When the hospital hadn't been able to reach McKenzie they'd called him, thinking he might be with her.

He would like to be with her. He should be with her. Instead, he'd sat through the last meeting before the Valentine's Day dance. They had everything under control and the event should be a great fund-raiser.

But where was McKenzie?

He was just getting ready to pull out of her driveway when her car came down the street and turned in.

"What are you doing here?" she asked, getting out of her car. "It's almost ten."

Yeah, he should have gone home. He didn't have to tell her tonight. Nothing would have been lost by her not finding out about the man until the next morning.

"I was worried about you."

"I'm fine."

"I'll go, then. I was just concerned when you didn't answer your phone."

"Sorry. I had my ringer turned off. I was at my mother's."

Her mother that he'd not met yet.

"She's getting married."

"Married?"

"Seems after all this time she's met the man of her dreams."

"You don't sound very happy about it."

She shrugged. "He's growing on me."

"Someone I know?"

"Unlikely. He just opened up the new health-food store on the square."

"Yves St. Claire?"

Her brows veed. "That's him. You know him?"

"I met him a few days after he opened the store. Great place he has there. Seems like a nice enough fellow."

"And?"

"And what?"

"Doesn't he seem too young for my mother?"

"I've never met your mother so I wouldn't know, but age is just a number."

"That's what she said."

"If I were younger than you, would it matter, McKenzie?"

"For our intents and purposes, I suppose that depends on how much younger. I don't mess with jailbait."

He laughed, leaned back against his car. "Glad I have a few years on you, then."

"Do you want to come inside?"

Relief washed over him. "I thought you'd never ask."

February the thirteenth fell on a Friday and McKenzie was convinced that the day truly was a bad-luck day.

Today was it. The end of her two months with Lance.

She'd promised herself there would be no fuss, no muss, just a quick and painless goodbye. He had his dance tomorrow night and no doubt by next week he'd have a new love interest.

But she couldn't quite convince herself of that.

Something in the way Lance looked at her made her think he wouldn't quickly replace her but might instead take some time to get over her.

Unfortunately, she might require that time, too.

Lots and lots of recovery time, though perhaps not the three decades' worth her mother had taken to blossom into a woman in love.

Her mother was in love. And loved.

Over the past several days McKenzie had been fitted for a maid-of-honor dress and had met Yves's best friend for his tux fitting. Her mother was getting married at a local church in a small, simple ceremony the following day.

"You're not planning to see me at all tonight?" Lance asked.

She shook her head. "My mother's wedding-rehearsal dinner is tonight."

"I could go with you."

"That would be a bad idea."

"Why?"

"Our last night together and we go to a wedding rehearsal? Think about it. That's just all kinds of wrong. Plus, I don't want you there, Lance."

He winced and she almost retracted her words. Part of her did want him there. Another part knew the sooner they parted the sooner she could get back to the regularly scheduled program of her life. Her time with Lance had been a nice interlude from reality.

"I should tell you that Yves invited me to the wedding."

"I don't want you there," she said.

"I'll keep that in mind." Without another word, he left her office.

McKenzie's heart shuddered at the soft closing of her office door as if the noise had echoed throughout the building.

She went to her mother's rehearsal dinner, smiled and performed her role as maid of honor. Truth was, watching her mother and Yves left her heart aching.

Feeling a little bereft at the thought she was soon to be single again.

Which was ridiculous.

She liked being single.

She thrived on being single.

She didn't want to be like her parents.

Only watching her mother glow, hearing her happy laughter, maybe she wouldn't mind being a little like her mother.

McKenzie got home a little after eleven. She'd not heard from Lance all evening. She'd half expected him to be waiting in her driveway.

No, more than half. She had expected him to be there.

That he wasn't left her feeling deflated.

Their last night together and they weren't together.

Would never be together again.

Sleep didn't come easily but unfortunately her tears did.

This was exactly why she should never have agreed to more than a month with him. Anything more was just too messy.

Lance sat in the fourth pew back on the groom's side. There were only about fifty or so people in the church when the music started and the groom and his best man joined the preacher at the front of the building. The music changed and a smiling McKenzie came down the aisle. Her gaze remained locked on the altar, as if she was afraid to look around. Maybe she was.

Maybe she had been serious in that she really hadn't wanted him to attend. Certainly, she hadn't contacted him last night. He'd checked his phone several times, thinking she might. She hadn't. He'd told himself that was a good thing, that McKenzie sticking to their original agreement made it easier for him to do so too.

Their two months was over.

The music changed and everyone stood, turned to watch the bride walk down the aisle to her groom.

Lance had never met McKenzie's mother, but he would have recognized the older version of McKenzie anywhere. Same green eyes. Same fine bone structure.

Seeing McKenzie made his insides ache.

Part of him wanted to ask her for more time, for another day, another week, another month.

But he couldn't.

Wouldn't.

He'd vowed to Shelby that he'd remain committed to her memory.

To spend more time with McKenzie would be wrong.

He wasn't free to be with her and never would be.

"You invited Dad?" McKenzie whispered, thinking her knees might buckle as she took her mother's bouquet from her.

Her mother's smile was full of merriment, but she didn't answer, just turned back to her groom to exchange her vows.

The exchange of wedding vows was brief and beautiful. McKenzie cried as her mother read the vows she'd written for a man she'd known for less than two months.

Less than the time McKenzie had been dating Lance.

McKenzie outright wept when Yves said his vows back

to her mother. Okay, so if the man loved her mother all his days the way he loved her today, he and McKenzie would get along just fine and her mother was a lucky woman.

The preacher announced the happy couple as Mr. and Mrs. Yves St. Clair and presented them to their guests.

A few photos were taken, then the reception began. McKenzie spotted Lance talking to a tall blonde someone had told her earlier was Yves's cousin. A deep green pain stabbed her, but she refused to acknowledge it or him. She headed toward her father, who was downing a glass of something alcoholic.

"I can't believe you are here."

He frowned into his empty glass. "She invited me."

"You didn't have to come."

His gaze met hers. "Sure I did. Today is a big day for me, too."

"Freedom from alimony?" she said drily.

For the first time in a long time her father's smile was real and reached his eyes. "Exactly."

"She seems really happy."

That had her father pausing and glancing toward her mother. "Yeah, she does. Good for her."

"What about you? Where is your wife?"

He shrugged. "At home, I imagine."

He excused himself and went and joined the conversation with Lance and the blonde. No doubt he'd have the blonde cornered in just a few minutes.

He must have because Lance walked up shortly afterward to where McKenzie stood.

"You look very beautiful," he said quietly.

Okay, so a smart girl wouldn't let him see how his words warmed her insides. A smart girl would play it cool. McKenzie tried. "Cecilia works wonders."

"She is indeed talented."

Their conversation was stilted, awkward. The conversation of former lovers who didn't know what to say to each other.

"I see you met my father," she said to fill the silence.

Shock registered on Lance's face. "That was your father?"

McKenzie laughed at his surprise. "Yes. Sorry he moved in on Yves's cousin while you were talking her up."

"I wasn't talking her up," he replied. "And, for the record, had I been interested in her no one would have moved in, including your father." He glanced around until his gaze lit on where her father still chatted with the blonde, who laughed a little too flirtatiously. "Isn't he married?"

She nodded. "Fidelity isn't his thing. I've mentioned that before."

Lance's expression wasn't pleasant. "Seems odd for him to be here, at your mother's wedding."

"I thought the same thing, but my mother invited him and he came. They are a bit weird that way. Something else I've mentioned."

Lance's gaze met McKenzie's and locked for a few long seconds before he glanced at his watch as if pressed for time. "Sorry to rush off, but I've got to head out to help with the Valentine's Day dance tonight."

"Oh. I forgot." Had her disappointment that he wasn't going to stay for a while shown? Of course it had.

He reached out, touched her cheek. "McKenzie, there's so much I could say to you."

"But?"

"But you already know everything I'd say."

"Not everything."

His brow rose and she shook her head. Now wasn't the time to ask him about Shelby. That time had come and gone.

Apparently he agreed because he said, "It's been fun."

She nodded, hoping the tears she felt prickling her eyes didn't burst free.

"Your car door was unlocked and I left something for you in the front seat of your car."

Her gaze lifted to his. "What? Why would you do that?"

"Just a little something for Valentine's Day."

He'd gotten her a gift for Valentine's Day? But they'd ended things the day before. She had not bought him the standard card. "I didn't get you anything."

"You didn't need to. Our two months is finished, just as we are." He glanced at his watch again. "Goodbye, McKenzie." Then, right there in the reception hall in front of her mother, her father and her brand-new stepfather, Lance kissed her.

Not a quick peck but a real kiss. Not a dragged-out one but one jam-packed with emotion all the same. One that demanded the same emotion back from her.

McKenzie blinked up at him. He looked as if he was about to say something but instead shook his head and left.

"Who was that man, McKenzie?" her mother asked, immediately joining her as Lance exited the building.

"That's what I want to know," her father practically bellowed. "Why was he kissing you?"

"Why is he leaving?" Her mother asked the more pressing question.

"He's just someone I work with," she mumbled, not wanting to discuss Lance.

"She gets that from you," her mother told her father. "The idea she's supposed to kiss people she works with."

"Violet," her father began, crossing his arms and giving her a sour look.

But her mother seemed to shake off her thoughts and smiled. "Come, let me introduce you to your much younger, more virile and loyal replacement."

"Sure took you long enough," her father gibed.

"Some of us are more choosy than others."

McKenzie watched her parents walk away together, bickering back and forth. It wasn't even six in the evening and exhaustion hit her.

Much, much later, after she'd waved sparklers at her mother and Yves's exit, McKenzie gathered up her belongings from the church classroom where the bridal party had gotten ready.

When she got into her car, her gaze immediately went to the passenger floorboard where she saw a vase full of red roses. On the passenger seat was a gift box. Chocolates?

She doubted it due to the odd box size. She ripped open the package, and gave a trembling smile at what was inside.

A new pair of running shoes.

CHAPTER THIRTEEN

"YOU'RE NOT RIGHT, you know."

McKenzie didn't argue with her best friend. Cecilia was correct and they both knew it. Then again, one didn't argue with a person streaking hair color through one's hair.

"I think you should talk to him."

"Who said this was about him?" Okay, so maybe she was feeling more argumentative than she should be.

Cecilia's gaze met McKenzie's in the large salon mirror in front of her styling chair. "You're still upset about your mother getting hitched? I thought you were over that."

"I am over that." How could she not be when her mother was happier than McKenzie recalled her ever being? When she'd morphed into an energetic, productive person who suddenly seemed to have her act together?

Yves had taken her to South America to a bird-watching resort for their honeymoon. Since they'd returned her mother seemed as happy as a lark, working at the health-food store with her new husband.

This from a woman who'd never really held a job.

"Then it has to be Lance."

"Why does it have to be Lance?"

"The reason you're lost in your thoughts and moping around like a lovesick puppy? Who else would it be?"

"I'm not," she denied with way too much gusto.

"Sure you are."

"I meant I'm not a lovesick puppy," she countered, because at least that much was true.

Cecilia laughed. "Keep telling yourself that, girlfriend, and maybe you'll convince one of us."

McKenzie didn't say anything, just sat in the chair while Cecilia dabbed more highlight color onto her hair, then wrapped the strand in aluminum foil.

"Have you tossed out the roses yet?"

What did it matter if she still had the roses Lance had given her on Valentine's Day? They still had a little color to them.

"I'm not answering that."

"It's been a month. They're dead. Let them go."

"I thought I might try my hand at making potpourri."

"Sure you did." Cecilia had the audacity to laugh as she tucked another wet strand of hair into a tinfoil packet. "What about the shoes?"

"What about them?"

"Don't play dumb with me. I've known you too long. Have you worn them yet?"

That was the problem with best friends. They had known you too long and too well.

"I've put them on," she admitted, not clarifying that she'd put them on a dozen times, staring at them, wondering what he'd meant by giving her running shoes. "They're a perfect fit."

"I wouldn't have expected otherwise. He pays attention to details."

Lance did pay attention to details. Like the fact she ran away when things got sticky. Then again, he hadn't tried to convince her not to. Not once had he mentioned anything beyond their seeing each other on Valentine's Day. If she'd agreed, would he have asked for more? No matter how many times she asked herself that question, she couldn't convince herself that he would have. She wasn't the only one who ran.

Maybe she should have gotten him a pair of running shoes, too.

She bit the inside of her lower lip. "You think I messed up letting him go, don't you?"

Cecilia's look was full of amusement. "If you were any quicker on the uptake I'd have to call you Einstein."

"It wasn't just my choice, you know. He walked away that night at my mother's rehearsal."

"He gave you roses and running shoes."

Yeah, he had.

"Running shoes? What kind of a gift is that anyway?"

"The kind that says he knows you better than you think he does. You're a runner—physically, mentally, emotionally. He also gave you red roses. What does that say?"

"Not what you're implying. He never told me that he loved me."

"Did you want him to?"

"I don't know."

"Sure you do." Cecilia pulled another strand of hair loose, coated it in dye, then wrapped it.

"He was in love with a woman who died. I can't compete with a ghost."

"She's gone. She's no longer any competition."

"Cecilia!"

"I don't mean to be crude, McKenzie, but if he's in love with a woman who is no longer around, well, she's not a real threat. Not unless you let her be."

"He never even mentioned her to me."

"There are lots of things you still haven't told him. That's what the rest of your lives are for."

"He and I agreed to a short-term relationship."

"You didn't have a signed contract. Terms can change."

"Ouch!" McKenzie yelped when Cecilia pulled a piece of hair too tightly.

"Sorry." But the gleam in her eyes warned that she might have done it on purpose. "You could have kept seeing him. You should have kept seeing him."

"He didn't want to go beyond our two months any more than I did."

"Sure you didn't. That's why you're miserable now that you're not with him anymore."

"I'm not miserable," McKenzie lied. "Besides, I see him at work."

"How's that?"

"Awkward. Strange. As bad as I was afraid it would be. I knew I shouldn't become involved with a coworker."

"So why did you?"

"Because…because I couldn't not."

Cecilia's face lit with excitement that McKenzie had finally caught on. "Exactly. That should tell you everything you need to know about how you feel about the man. Why you are so intent on denying that you miss him makes no sense to me."

"I miss him," she admitted. "There, does that make you happy? I miss Lance. I miss the way he looks, the way he smiles, the way he smells, the way he tastes. I miss everything about him."

Cecilia spun the chair to face her straight on, her eyes full of sympathy. "Girl, how can you not see what is so obvious?"

McKenzie's rib cage contracted tightly around everything in her chest. "You think I'm in love with him."

"Aren't you?"

McKenzie winced. She wasn't. Couldn't be. She shouldn't be.

She was.

"What am I going to do?"

"Well, you are your mother's daughter. Maybe you should grab the happiness you want instead of being afraid it's always going to be just outside your grasp."

All these years she'd not wanted to be like her mother, but her mother had been happy, had been choosing to be single, but not out of fear of love. If her mother, who'd borne the brunt of so much hurt, could love, could trust, why couldn't McKenzie?

If her mother could put her heart out there, be in a committed relationship, find happiness, why couldn't McKenzie?

Maybe she wasn't like her father. Maybe she wasn't like her mother either.

Maybe she was tiny pieces of both, could learn from their mistakes, learn from their successes and be a better person.

Right now, she wasn't a better person. Right now, she didn't even feel like a whole person. She felt like only half a person, with the other half of her missing.

Lance.

"I want him back," she admitted, causing Cecilia's eyes to widen with satisfaction.

"Good. Now, how are you going to make it happen?"

"He didn't want more than our two months, Cecilia. He was as insistent on our ending point as I was," she mused. "I wasn't the only one who let us end at two months. He didn't fight to hang on to me." He hadn't. He'd walked away without a backward glance. "His heart belongs to another woman."

"Another woman who can't have him," Cecilia reminded her. "If you want Lance back, then you don't worry about whether or not he's fighting for you. You fight for him. You show him you want him in your life. Show him how much he means to you."

She did want Lance back and, Lord help her, she wanted

to fight for him, to show him she missed him and wanted him in her life.

"How am I supposed to do that?"

Cecilia's gaze shifted to the back of a flyer posted on the salon's front door. A flyer someone from Celebration Graduation had dropped by a week or so ago, advertising a St. Patrick's Day show at the Senior Citizen Center.

"I have the perfect idea."

McKenzie could see her friend mentally rubbing her hands together in glee. "Why do I get the feeling I'm not going to like this?"

Lance shoved the giant four-leaf clover to the middle of the stage, trying to decide if the light was going to reflect off the glittery surface correctly or if he should reposition the stage prop.

"That looks great there," one of the other volunteers called out, answering his silent question.

He finished arranging props on the stage, then went to the room they were using as a dressing room to get ready for the actual show. He was emceeing.

The event hadn't been a planned Celebration Graduation fund-raiser, but the Senior Citizen Center had approached him with the idea and the earnest desire to help with the project. How could he say no?

Besides, he'd needed something to focus on besides the gaping hole in his chest.

He should be used to having a gaping hole in his chest.

Hadn't he had one since he'd been a seventeen-year-old kid and the love of his life had been killed in a car accident?

Only had Shelby really been the love of his life? Or had she just been his first love and their relationship had never been able to run its natural course to its inevitable conclusion?

Which was his fault.

He winced at his thoughts. Why was he allowing such negativity into his head?

It had been his fault Shelby was no longer alive. He'd promised her that her death wouldn't be in vain, that her life wouldn't be forgotten. He'd vowed to keep her alive in his heart and mind. Wasn't that why he did the volunteer work?

Wasn't that why he headed up Celebration Graduation?

So that no other teen had to go through what he and Shelby had gone through?

So that there were other options in teens' lives besides making bad choices on graduation night?

If only their school had offered a Celebration Graduation program. If only he and Shelby had gone to the event rather than the party they'd been at. If only he hadn't given in to peer pressure and drunk. If only he'd not let her drink, not let her get into that car for him to drive them home that night.

If only.

If only.

If only.

Hadn't he spent a lifetime playing out if-onlys in his head? What good had they ever done? He couldn't go back to that night, couldn't bring Shelby back. All he could do was carry on and make a difference in other teens' lives.

He did make a difference in other teens' lives. Both at his job where he counseled and encouraged teens to make good decisions and with Celebration Graduation.

Shelby would be proud of the man he'd become.

At least, he thought she would.

That's what kept him going, knowing that he was living his life to make a difference for others.

He couldn't let anything, anyone get in the way of that.

"There's a full house out there already," one of the other cast members told him, taking one last look in the mirror before moving to the doorway. "This was a great idea, Dr. Spencer."

"I can't take the credit. The Senior Citizen Center approached me," he admitted.

"Well, I'd say they've sold out the show," Lanette said, peeping through a curtain to look at the crowd. "There's only a few seats left and it's still a good fifteen minutes before showtime."

Lance had called the cast members from the Christmas show and gotten them on board to do a St. Patrick's Day show. They'd kept it simple, doing numbers that they all already knew, but that would be fun for the audience. Lance had even convinced a magician to come in and do a few tricks between sets. If the guy worked out, Lance hoped to have him perform on graduation night at the kids' lock-in to help pass their time in a fun way.

Seven arrived and Lance went out onto their makeshift stage. He welcomed the crowd, apologized to the ones standing in the back of the room, but applauded them on participating in something that was for such a worthy cause.

He moved to the side of the stage. Four of the female performers came out onstage, holding sparkly four-leaf clovers the size of dinner plates. The performers changed and a male singer crooned out a love ballad that had Lance's throat clogging up a little.

He didn't want to think about Shelby. He didn't want to think about McKenzie.

He couldn't stop thinking about either.

The crowd cheered each performance.

They finished the first half of the show, went to the back to grab a drink and change costumes while the magician did his show. Lance found himself laughing at some of the tricks and trying to figure out how a few others were done. The crowd loved the show. Soon the singers were back onstage and sang a few more songs. Lanette had the lead in the next number and took the stage with a bright smile.

"Okay, folks, this is a little different from what's on your program, but sometimes the best performances are the unexpected, impromptu ones," Lanette began, causing Lance to frown.

He was unaware of any changes to their schedule and certainly there weren't any planned impromptu performances that he knew of.

That's when he saw her.

McKenzie, wearing her sparkly green dress that she must have had hidden beneath a jacket for him to have not noticed her before because she glimmered with every step she took toward the stage.

What was she doing?

But even before Lanette handed her the microphone, he knew.

McKenzie was going to sing.

The question was why.

And why was his heart beating so crazily in his chest with excitement over what she was about to do when he had no right to feel that excitement?

To feel that joy that McKenzie was there?

Any moment McKenzie expected her heels to give way and she would fall flat on her face. Definitely she was more comfortable in her running shoes than the three-inch heels she'd chosen to wear because Cecilia had told her they made her legs look phenomenal.

Who cared how good her legs looked if she was flat on her butt from her feet going out from under her?

Or maybe it was because her knees were shaking that she feared falling.

Her knees were shaking, knocking together like clackers.

Why was she doing this? Wouldn't a simple phone call

or text message have sufficed? No, she'd had to go along with Cecilia's idea that she had to do something big, something totally out of character to convince Lance she was playing for keeps.

Cecilia had arranged a voice coach who'd worked with McKenzie every night that week. Cecilia had called a client who happened to be one of the female singers in the show and arranged for McKenzie's surprise performance. Lanette had been thrilled to help because she'd seen McKenzie and Lance save the mayor's life and had thought them a perfect couple even back then.

Now it was all up to McKenzie.

She hated people looking at her and the entire room's eyes were all trained on her, waiting to see what she was going to do. To see if she was going to cry or scream out like her parents.

No, that's not why they were here. That's not why they were looking at her. They were here for entertainment. Entertainment she was about to add to, and perhaps not in a good way.

She couldn't sing.

A week with a voice coach wasn't going to fix that. A year with a voice coach couldn't.

But she'd learned what her voice's strengths were and what her weaknesses were. Her performance wasn't going to have any agents lining up to sign her, but hopefully her putting herself out there for him would impress a certain man enough for him to rethink two months, for him to open up his heart and let her inside, to at least give her, give them, a chance.

The music started up as she made her way up the steps to the stage. One step. Two steps. Three steps. On the stage without falling. Yes, now, if she could just stay upright during her song, she totally had this.

She made her way over to Lance, smiled at him suggestively as she ran her finger along his shirt collar. His body heat lured her in, making her want to touch him for real, but common sense said she was on a stage, everyone was watching, the show must go on and this wasn't that kind of show.

Taking a deep breath first that she hoped the microphone didn't pick up, she broke into a song about going after what she wanted and making it hers.

If he walked away from her, she'd look a fool.

She'd feel a fool.

But, even more, he might not forgive her for interfering in his show.

Still, she agreed with Cecilia. She had to make a grand gesture to show Lance that she was serious about wanting him in her life, that she was willing to take risks where he was concerned, that she'd fight for him.

That she'd sing for him.

So she sang.

His eyes searched hers and she couldn't quite read his expression.

Fine. She was going to do this, was going to put her heart into it, and whatever happened happened.

She played her eyes at him, did her best to be sultry and seductive without being trashy, and felt a huge weight lift off her when Lance grinned.

Thank God. At least he wasn't going to have her look a fool on the stage.

To those in the audience he looked believable. To McKenzie he looked more beautiful than anything she'd ever seen.

She finished the song.

Shaking his head, he wrapped her into his arms, spun her around, and kissed her forehead.

"Ladies and gentlemen, give it up for Dr. McKenzie Sanders."

The room filled with applause.

"Bow," Lance whispered, squeezing her hand.

Feeling a bit silly, she did so.

He led her off the stage and round to the back as Lanette took to the stage again to perform another song.

"What are you doing here?" he asked the second they were out of sight of the audience.

Ouch. Not exactly what she'd hoped to hear him say. Then again, what had she expected? For him to immediately know what her song had meant? He was a man. Sometimes men had to be hit over the head with the obvious for them to recognize the truth, or so her best friend had told her repeatedly.

"I'm here to sing for you."

His brow lifted. "I thought you didn't like singing?"

"I don't."

"Then why?"

"Because I want to be a part of the things you enjoy. Two months wasn't enough time. I want more. I need more."

He considered her a moment, glanced at the other crew members who were backstage, then pulled her toward the back. "Obviously we need to talk, but this isn't the time or the place."

"Obviously," she agreed, knowing the other cast members were watching them curiously.

"I have to be there for the last song. All the cast members will be onstage for it. I give my thanks to the cast and the Senior Citizen Center, and then we'll take our bows."

"I can wait."

The others lined up to take the stage as soon as Lanette's number ended. Lance glanced toward her and looked torn.

"Go. I'll be here when you're finished."

"You're sure?"

"In case you haven't figured it out just by my being here, I'm planning to stick around, Lance. Two months wasn't enough time. At least, not for me. Unless... You're not seeing anyone else, are you?"

She'd not even considered that he might already be seeing someone else. She couldn't imagine it. Not with the way he looked at her. But sometimes people did stupid things.

"There's no one else, McKenzie. Just you."

Although his face went a ghostly white at his own words, they put such joy into her heart that she threw her arms around him and kissed him, letting every bit of feeling inside her show in her kiss.

One of the other singers cleared his throat, reminding them that Lanette's number was coming to an end.

"Sorry," McKenzie apologized, then took it back. "No, I'm not sorry. Not that I kissed you anyway. Just that I haven't kissed you every night for the past month. I've missed you."

Lance pulled away from McKenzie without saying anything.

He'd already said enough.

He'd said there was no one else.

Just her.

How could he have said that?

His insides shook.

A crushing weight settled onto his chest.

One that made breathing difficult, much less saying anything as he took to the stage.

He went through the motions, had the cast bowing at the appropriate times, the crowd applauding, and the cast applauding the Senior Citizen Center. But he couldn't keep his mind on what he was doing, no matter how much he tried.

Just her. Just McKenzie.

Not Shelby.

How could he have said *Just McKenzie*?

How could he feel that?

He owed Shelby his dedication, his life, because he'd taken hers.

Then it was time for Lance to thank everyone for attending and for their donations to Celebration Graduation.

Only when he went to thank them did more words spill out than he'd meant to say. Words he'd never spoken out loud. Not ever.

"I've had people ask me in the past why I'm so passionate about Celebration Graduation," he began, staring out into the audience without really seeing anyone. "Most of the time I come up with an answer about how I believe in the cause and want to do my part. The truth goes much deeper than that. The truth is that I'm the reason programs such as Celebration Graduation need to exist. At the end of my junior year my girlfriend, who'd just graduated from high school, was killed in a car crash because I made the bad decision to drive while under the influence of alcohol. I lost control of the car and hit a tree. We were both airlifted to a trauma hospital. She died later that night."

McKenzie covered her mouth with her hand.

Oh, God. She should have known, should have figured out the truth behind Shelby's death. Only how could she have?

"So the truth is that my passion about Celebration Graduation, which gives teenagers an alternative to how they spend their graduation night, comes from my own past mistakes. I lived through what I hope to prevent from ever happening again." Lance's voice broke and for a moment McKenzie didn't think he was going to be able to say more, but then he continued.

"Through Celebration Graduation I hope to keep Shelby's memory alive, to make her life, her death matter, for her to make a difference in others' lives because she was a very special person and would have done great things in the world had she gotten the chance."

Tears ran down McKenzie's face. Dear Lord, she was devastated by the pain inside him. By the guilt inside him. She could hear it wrenched from him. He had loved Shelby.

He did love Shelby.

Lance's heart belonged to another. Irrevocably.

"Thank you for being here today, for helping me keep Shelby alive in my heart, and for making a difference in our youth's lives through this wonderful program."

At first there was a moment of silence, as if the audience wasn't sure whether to applaud or just sit there, then a single person clapped, then the room burst into applause.

McKenzie watched Lance say something to Lanette. She nodded, and he disappeared off the opposite side of the stage.

McKenzie waited at the side of the stage, but Lance didn't reappear. After they'd mingled with the crowd, the other performers returned.

"He told me to tell you he was sorry but that he had to leave," Lanette told her in a low voice so the others couldn't hear.

"He left?" McKenzie's heart pounded. He'd left. How could he do that, knowing she was backstage? Knowing she'd come to fight for him?

But she knew.

She recognized exactly what he'd done, because it was something she excelled at.

He'd run.

CHAPTER FOURTEEN

LANCE KNELT BESIDE the grave, thinking himself crazy for being at a cemetery at this time of night. The show hadn't ended until after nine, and by the time he'd realized where he'd been headed it had been almost eleven.

He hadn't consciously decided to go to Shelby's grave, but it's where his car had taken him. Maybe it was where he needed to go to put things into proper perspective.

Because for a few minutes he'd allowed himself to look into McKenzie's eyes while she'd sung to him and he'd acknowledged the truth.

He was in love with her.

Right or wrong, he loved her.

And she loved him. Perhaps he'd always known she felt that way, had seen the truth in her eyes when she'd looked at him, had felt the truth in her touch, in her kiss.

She looked at him the way her mother looked at Yves. The way his mother looked at his father. The way his grandmother looked at his grandfather.

Tonight, while she'd sung to him, McKenzie had looked at him with her heart shining through every word.

In the past she'd fought that feeling, had been determined not to allow herself to be hurt by making the mistakes her parents had made. Tonight she'd put everything on the line and he'd felt exhilarated to realize she was there for him, that she loved him and wanted him.

Then reality had set in.

He wasn't free to accept her love, to return her love. He'd vowed his love to another he owed everything to.

And he'd resented his vow. He'd resented Shelby.

The guilt of that resentment sickened him.

"Forgive me, Shelby. Forgive me for that night. Forgive me for not keeping you safe," he pleaded over the grave, much as he had many times in the past.

"Forgive me for still being here when you're not."

Wasn't that the crux of the matter?

He'd lived and Shelby hadn't.

How many times had he wished he could give his life for hers?

Standing at this very graveside, he'd vowed that his heart would always belong to her, that he'd never love another, never marry another. Even at seventeen he hadn't been so naive as to think he'd spend his life alone, so he had dated over the years, had been in relationships, but not once had he ever been tempted to sway from his promise to Shelby.

Until tonight.

Until McKenzie.

With McKenzie everything had changed.

With McKenzie he wanted everything.

Because he really did want McKenzie.

"Forgive me, Shelby. Forgive me for the way I feel about McKenzie. You'd like her, you know. She's a lot like what you might have been at her age. She loves to run, just as you did. And she's a doctor, just as you always planned to be. And I love her, just as I planned to always love you."

Guilt ripped through him.

He swiped at moisture on his face.

This was crazy. Why was he here? Then again, he felt crazy. He'd told everyone at the Senior Citizen Center his most guarded secret. He'd told them he'd essentially murdered Shelby.

The authorities hadn't seen it that way. Neither had Shelby's parents or his own family. She'd been eighteen to his seventeen. She'd been caught drinking in the past, he'd been a stupid kid trying to fit in with her older friends, but he knew that he shouldn't have been drinking or driving.

Memories of that night assailed him. For years he'd blocked them from his mind, not wanting to remember.

Shelby dancing. Shelby smiling and laughing. Shelby so full of life. And liquor. She'd been full of that, too.

She'd wanted more, had been going to take his car to get more, and he'd argued with her.

Even with being under the influence himself, he'd known she'd been in no shape to drive. Unfortunately, neither had he been and he'd known it, refusing to give her his keys.

She'd taken off running into the darkness, calling out over her shoulder that if he wouldn't take her, she'd just run there.

He should have let her. She'd have run herself sober.

Instead, to the teasing of her friends that he couldn't control his girlfriend, he'd climbed into his car and driven down the road to pick her up.

But he hadn't been taking her to the liquor store when he'd wrecked the car.

He'd been taking her home.

They'd been arguing, her saying she should have known he was a baby, rather than a man.

He'd been mad, had denied her taunts, reminded her of just how manly she'd said he was earlier that evening, and in the blink of the eye she'd grabbed at the steering wheel and he'd lost control of his car and hit the tree.

The rest had come in bits and pieces.

Waking up, not realizing he'd wrecked the car. The smells of oil, gas and blood.

That was the first time he'd realized blood had such a

strong odor. His car had been full of it. His blood. Shelby's blood.

He'd become aware of people outside the car, working to free them from the crumpled metal, but then he'd lost consciousness again until they'd been pulling him from the car.

Shelby had still been inside.

"I can't leave her," he'd told them.

"We've got her, son," a rescue worker had said. "We're taking you both to the hospital."

"Tell her I love her," he'd said. "That I will always love her."

"We will, son. They're putting her in the helicopter right now, but I'll see to it she gets the message."

"Tell her now. Please. Tell her now." He'd tried to get free, to go to her, but his body hadn't worked, and he'd never got to tell her. He had no idea if the rescue worker had carried through with his promise or not.

But as soon as Lance had been released from the hospital, he'd told Shelby himself.

Kneeling exactly where he currently knelt.

He'd been guilt-ridden then. He was just as guilt-ridden now.

"I'm so sorry, Shelby. I love her. In ways I didn't know I could love, I love McKenzie."

He continued to talk, saying all the things that were in his heart.

For the first time peace came over Lance. Peace and self-forgiveness. Oh, there was a part of him that would never completely let go of the guilt he felt that he'd made such bad choices that night, but whether it was the late hour or his own imagination he felt Shelby's presence, felt her forgiveness, her desire for him to let go and move on with his life.

Was he being self-delusional? Believing what he wanted to believe because he wanted McKenzie?

"I need a sign, Shelby. Give me a sign that you really do forgive me," he pleaded into the darkness.

That was when he looked up and saw a ghost.

McKenzie couldn't stay in the shadows any longer. For the past half hour she had leaned against a large headstone, crying, not knowing whether to make her presence known or not. She hadn't purposely tried to keep her presence from him initially. He just had been so lost in his thoughts, in his confessions that he hadn't noticed her.

Lance had run away from her.

Only he loved her. She'd known he loved her even before she'd heard his heart-wrenching words, and she hadn't been willing to give him up without a fight. Especially not to someone who'd been gone for over fifteen years.

She'd listened to him, cried with him and for him from afar, and had prayed for him to find forgiveness, to be able to let his guilt go.

When he'd asked for a sign she'd swear she'd felt a hard shove on her back, making her stumble forward, almost falling in the process.

"Shelby?"

Her heart broke at the anguish in his voice. "It's McKenzie, Lance."

Wiping at his eyes, he stood. "McKenzie? What are you doing here?"

"I followed you."

"You followed me from the Senior Citizen Center?"

"It wasn't difficult as slowly as you drive." Which she now finally understood. He liked his fast sports car, but never got it up over the speed limit.

"I didn't see you."

"I didn't think you had. I sat in my car for a few minutes after you first got here. I realized where you were going and was going to give you privacy, but it's after midnight and we're at a cemetery and I'll admit I got a little freaked out, sitting in my car by myself."

"You shouldn't be here, McKenzie."

Yeah, he might think that.

"You're wrong. This is exactly where I should be. Right beside you."

"I don't understand."

"You love me," she told him. "And I love you. And maybe you love her, too, but she isn't here anymore." At least, McKenzie didn't think she was. That had been her imagination playing tricks on her when she'd felt that shove. "I am here, Lance. I used to be terrified that I'd make all the same mistakes my parents made, but I'm not anymore. I'm not like my father, although I may be more like my mother than I realized. You told me that my father did those things because he loved himself more than my mother or me."

"I shouldn't have said that, McKenzie."

"Sure you should have. You were right. But guess what, Lance Donovan Spencer? I love you that much. I love you enough to know that you are who I want, that you are the man I admire above all others, that you are the person I love enough to know that being faithful won't be a problem because I don't want anyone but you."

"Don't admire me, McKenzie. I'm not worthy. You heard what I admitted to back at the Senior Citizen Center."

"I heard and I love you all the more for it."

In the moonlight, she saw the confusion on his face. "How can you love me for something I detest myself for?"

"Because in the face of adversity you learned from the lessons life threw at you and you became a wonderful man who is constantly doing things for others, who is constantly trying to save others from the agony he suffers every day, from Shelby's fate."

"You make me sound like a hero. I'm not."

"To me, you are a hero. You are my hero, Lance. You're

the man who made me know what love is, both to feel and to receive it."

He closed his eyes.

"Don't try to tell me you don't love me, because I heard you say it," she warned. "But I already knew, deep down, I knew. That's why I sang to you, why I followed you. Because of love and my trust in that love."

"I don't deserve you."

"I'm stubborn and prideful and prone to run when things get sticky, but take a look at these." She raised one foot up off the ground. While she'd been sitting in her car, waiting for him to come back to his, she'd changed out of her heels and into the pair of running shoes he'd given her. "See these? My man gave them to me for Valentine's Day so I could run to him. He doesn't know it yet, but I have a pair for him in my car so, that way, the next time he runs, he can run to me, too."

"You knew I was going to run away tonight?"

"My singing is pretty bad. I wasn't expecting you to swoon with the sudden realization that everything was going to be perfect."

"Your singing was beautiful."

"I've heard of being blinded by love, but I'm pretty sure you must be tone-deaf from love."

"I do love you, McKenzie."

"I know."

"I made Shelby a promise."

"One you've kept all these years. It's time to let go. You asked Shelby to give you a sign, Lance. I'm that sign. The way we feel about each other." She wrapped her arms around him and leaned her forehead against his chin. "I don't need you to forget Shelby. She's part of what's made you into the man you are, the man I love, but you have to let the guilt go. You can't change the past, only the future. I want to be your future."

"What are you saying, McKenzie?"

"That I want a lot more than two months to see what the future holds for us."

Lance held the woman in his arms tightly to him. He couldn't believe she was here, that they were standing by Shelby's grave at midnight.

He couldn't believe McKenzie was laying her heart on the line, telling him how much she cared.

"If we do this," he warned, his heart pounding in his chest, "I'm never going to let you go, you do realize that?"

She snuggled closer to him and held on tight. "Maybe you weren't paying attention, but that's the idea."

EPILOGUE

"The emcee just winked at you."

McKenzie nodded at her mother. "Yep, he did."

"He has a disgusting habit of doing that," Cecilia accused with a shake of her head.

"You're just jealous," McKenzie teased her friend.

"Ha. I don't think so. My hunky boyfriend is Santa, baby," Cecilia countered, making McKenzie laugh.

"Yeah, yeah. Quit pulling rank just because Santa has the hots for you."

"I could dress as Santa if you're into that kind of thing," Yves offered Violet.

"Eww. Don't need to hear this." McKenzie put her fingers over her ears. "La-la-la. I'm finding my happy place, where I *didn't* just hear my stepdad offer to dress up as Santa to give my mom her kicks."

Yves waggled his brows and gave Violet a wink of her own. McKenzie's mother giggled in response. McKenzie just kept her hands over her ears, but she couldn't keep the smile from her face at how happy her mother was or how much in love the two newlyweds were.

"Ahem." Cecilia nudged her arm. "The emcee is trying to get your attention."

"He has my attention." And her heart. The past nine months had been amazing, full of life and happiness and embracing her feelings for Lance, with him embracing his feelings for her. Sure, there were moments when her old insecurities slipped through, but they were farther and farther apart. Just as Lance's moments of guilt were farther and farther apart.

He'd even been asked to speak at the local high school the week before graduation to talk to the kids about what had happened with Shelby. McKenzie had been so proud of him, of the way he'd opened up and shared with the kids his tragedy, how he'd lived his life trying to make amends, but one never really could. The Celebration Graduation committee had surprised Lance by setting up the Shelby Hanover Scholarship in her honor and had made the award to its first recipient following Lance's talk at the high school.

"Yeah, well, he's motioning for you to join him onstage," Cecilia pointed out. "He gonna have you croon for him again?"

"I hope not." McKenzie still didn't enjoy singing or having everyone's eyes on her, but the emcee aka the most wonderful man in the world truly was motioning her to come up onto the stage.

She got onto the stage. "Please tell me I'm not about to embarrass myself by singing some Christmas ditty."

Grinning, he shook his head. "You're not about to embarrass yourself by singing."

"Phew," she said. "That's a relief to everyone in the audience."

One of the performers brought over a chair and set it down behind where McKenzie stood next to Lance. She glanced around at the chair, then looked at Lance in question.

"Have a seat, McKenzie."

She eyed him curiously. "What's going on?"

The look in his eyes had her concerned. His grin had faded and he actually looked nervous.

"Lance?"

"Sit, please."

McKenzie sat, which must have cued the music because it started up the moment her bottom hit the seat.

When she caught the tune, she smiled.

All the performers came out onto the stage and began singing. Lance stood in front of her, his eyes full of love. When the song ended, she got to her feet and kissed him.

The crowd cheered.

"You have me, you know," she whispered, for his ears only.

"I sure hope so or I'm about to look like the world's biggest fool."

She arched a brow at him. "Lance?"

"Have a seat, McKenzie."

Her gaze met his and her mouth fell open as she sat back down.

A big smile on his face, Lance dropped to one knee, right there on the Coopersville Community Center's stage, with half the town watching.

"McKenzie, at this show last year you saved the mayor's life," Lance began. "But without knowing it, you saved mine, too."

McKenzie's eyes watered.

He wasn't doing this.

He *was* doing this.

"This past year has been the best of my life because I've spent it with you, but more than that you've helped me to be the person I was meant to be, to let go of things that needed to be let go of, and to embrace the aspects of life that needed to be embraced."

"Lance," she whispered, her hand shaking as he took it in his.

"I can't imagine my life without you in it every single day."

"You'll never have to," she promised.

"I'd like to make that official, get it in writing," he teased, drawing a laugh from their audience. "McKenzie, will you do me the honor of becoming my wife?"

McKenzie stared into the eyes of the man who'd taught her what it meant to love and be loved and felt her heart expand even further, so much so that she felt her chest bursting with love.

"Oh, yes." She nodded, watching as he slipped a diamond ring onto the third finger of her left hand.

He lifted her hand, kissed her fingers. "I love you, McKenzie."

"I love you, too, Lance."

Lance lifted her to her feet, kissed her.

The curtain fell, closing them off from the applauding audience.

"Merry Christmas, McKenzie."

"The merriest."

* * * * *

*If you enjoyed this story,
check out these other great reads from
Janice Lynn*

*SIZZLING NIGHTS WITH DR OFF-LIMITS
WINTER WEDDING IN VEGAS
NEW YORK DOC TO BLUSHING BRIDE
FLIRTING WITH THE DOC OF HER DREAMS*

All available now!

MILLS & BOON®
Hardback – November 2016

ROMANCE

Di Sione's Virgin Mistress	Sharon Kendrick
Snowbound with His Innocent Temptation	Cathy Williams
The Italian's Christmas Child	Lynne Graham
A Diamond for Del Rio's Housekeeper	Susan Stephens
Claiming His Christmas Consequence	Michelle Smart
One Night with Gael	Maya Blake
Married for the Italian's Heir	Rachael Thomas
Unwrapping His Convenient Fiancée	Melanie Milburne
Christmas Baby for the Princess	Barbara Wallace
Greek Tycoon's Mistletoe Proposal	Kandy Shepherd
The Billionaire's Prize	Rebecca Winters
The Earl's Snow-Kissed Proposal	Nina Milne
The Nurse's Christmas Gift	Tina Beckett
The Midwife's Pregnancy Miracle	Kate Hardy
Their First Family Christmas	Alison Roberts
The Nightshift Before Christmas	Annie O'Neil
It Started at Christmas...	Janice Lynn
Unwrapped by the Duke	Amy Ruttan
Hold Me, Cowboy	Maisey Yates
Holiday Baby Scandal	Jules Bennett

MILLS & BOON®
Large Print – November 2016

ROMANCE

Di Sione's Innocent Conquest	Carol Marinelli
A Virgin for Vasquez	Cathy Williams
The Billionaire's Ruthless Affair	Miranda Lee
Master of Her Innocence	Chantelle Shaw
Moretti's Marriage Command	Kate Hewitt
The Flaw in Raffaele's Revenge	Annie West
Bought by Her Italian Boss	Dani Collins
Wedded for His Royal Duty	Susan Meier
His Cinderella Heiress	Marion Lennox
The Bridesmaid's Baby Bump	Kandy Shepherd
Bound by the Unborn Baby	Bella Bucannon

HISTORICAL

The Unexpected Marriage of Gabriel Stone	Louise Allen
The Outcast's Redemption	Sarah Mallory
Claiming the Chaperon's Heart	Anne Herries
Commanded by the French Duke	Meriel Fuller
Unbuttoning the Innocent Miss	Bronwyn Scott

MEDICAL

Tempted by Hollywood's Top Doc	Louisa George
Perfect Rivals...	Amy Ruttan
English Rose in the Outback	Lucy Clark
A Family for Chloe	Lucy Clark
The Doctor's Baby Secret	Scarlet Wilson
Married for the Boss's Baby	Susan Carlisle

1016 GEN STD LP

MILLS & BOON®
Hardback – December 2016

ROMANCE

A Di Sione for the Greek's Pleasure	Kate Hewitt
The Prince's Pregnant Mistress	Maisey Yates
The Greek's Christmas Bride	Lynne Graham
The Guardian's Virgin Ward	Caitlin Crews
A Royal Vow of Convenience	Sharon Kendrick
The Desert King's Secret Heir	Annie West
Married for the Sheikh's Duty	Tara Pammi
Surrendering to the Vengeful Italian	Angela Bissell
Winter Wedding for the Prince	Barbara Wallace
Christmas in the Boss's Castle	Scarlet Wilson
Her Festive Doorstep Baby	Kate Hardy
Holiday with the Mystery Italian	Ellie Darkins
White Christmas for the Single Mum	Susanne Hampton
A Royal Baby for Christmas	Scarlet Wilson
Playboy on Her Christmas List	Carol Marinelli
The Army Doc's Baby Bombshell	Sue MacKay
The Doctor's Sleigh Bell Proposal	Susan Carlisle
The Baby Proposal	Andrea Laurence
Maid Under the Mistletoe	Maureen Child

MILLS & BOON®
Large Print – December 2016

ROMANCE

The Di Sione Secret Baby	Maya Blake
Carides's Forgotten Wife	Maisey Yates
The Playboy's Ruthless Pursuit	Miranda Lee
His Mistress for a Week	Melanie Milburne
Crowned for the Prince's Heir	Sharon Kendrick
In the Sheikh's Service	Susan Stephens
Marrying Her Royal Enemy	Jennifer Hayward
An Unlikely Bride for the Billionaire	Michelle Douglas
Falling for the Secret Millionaire	Kate Hardy
The Forbidden Prince	Alison Roberts
The Best Man's Guarded Heart	Katrina Cudmore

HISTORICAL

Sheikh's Mail-Order Bride	Marguerite Kaye
Miss Marianne's Disgrace	Georgie Lee
Her Enemy at the Altar	Virginia Heath
Enslaved by the Desert Trader	Greta Gilbert
Royalist on the Run	Helen Dickson

MEDICAL

The Prince and the Midwife	Robin Gianna
His Pregnant Sleeping Beauty	Lynne Marshall
One Night, Twin Consequences	Annie O'Neil
Twin Surprise for the Single Doc	Susanne Hampton
The Doctor's Forbidden Fling	Karin Baine
The Army Doc's Secret Wife	Charlotte Hawkes

MILLS & BOON®

Why shop at millsandboon.co.uk?

Each year, thousands of romance readers find their perfect read at millsandboon.co.uk. That's because we're passionate about bringing you the very best romantic fiction. Here are some of the advantages of shopping at www.millsandboon.co.uk:

* **Get new books first**—you'll be able to buy your favourite books one month before they hit the shops

* **Get exclusive discounts**—you'll also be able to buy our specially created monthly collections, with up to 50% off the RRP

* **Find your favourite authors**—latest news, interviews and new releases for all your favourite authors and series on our website, plus ideas for what to try next

* **Join in**—once you've bought your favourite books, don't forget to register with us to rate, review and join in the discussions

Visit **www.millsandboon.co.uk**
for all this and more today!